Ultimatum

Richard Rohmer

ULTIMATUM

CLARKE, IRWIN & COMPANY LIMITED / TORONTO / VANCOUVER

ISBN 0-7720-0618-0

1 2 3 4 5   BP   77 76 75 74 73

Printed in Canada

To my beautiful daughters,
Cathy and Ann

PORTER, Rt. Hon. Robert Maitland, P.C., Q.C., M.P., Prime Minister of Canada since August, 1980; b. Winnipeg, 7 May, 1935; s. Wilfred Martin and Nora (Carter) P.; B.A. University of Manitoba, 1956; LL.B. University of Alberta, 1960; LL.M., 1967; called to Bar of Alberta, 1960; m. Min Carpenter, 1967 (deceased); no children; practised law with Simpson & Crane, Calgary, 1960-66; mem. law firm Porter & Smith, Inuvik, 1966-74; elected to House of Commons, 1974; Minister of Energy, Mines and Resources, 1977-80. Member Arctic Institute of North America, the Law Society of Alberta and the Northwest Territories. Publications: A Proud People, 1969; Reconquering Our Land, 1971. Recreations: riding, fishing, snowshoeing. Address: Prime Minister's Residence, 24 Sussex Drive, Ottawa, Canada.

——————————————, President U.S.; b. Houston, Tex., Sept. 17, 1921; s. James Howard and Margaret (Stafford) B.; LL.B. University of Texas; m. Jennifer Harley, May 3, 1949; children — James Everett, Marian Stafford (Mrs. Walter Morton). Mem. law firm Whitfield, Harley, Wilkinson & Steele, Houston, 1949-53; atty for Masefield, Warfield, Hamilton & Smith, ind. oil operators, Ft. Worth, 1953-60; mem. 87th, 88th, 89th U.S. Congresses; senator, 1967-71; elected President of United States, Nov., 1976, took office, Jan. 21, 1977. Served to lt. col., U.S.A.F., 1941-45, ETO. Decorated DFC, Air medal with three oak leaf clusters. Democrat. Home: The White House, 1600 Pennsylvania Ave. N.W., Washington.

Day One

9:00 a.m., EDT = 8:00 a.m., CDT = 7:00 a.m., MDT

The Prime Minister's intercom buzzed. His secretary sounded excited. "Prime Minister, the President of the United States is calling. The President himself is on the line."

Robert Porter hesitated a moment, then he picked up the telephone.

"Good morning, Mr. President. To what do I owe the honour of being called by the President of the United States at nine o'clock on a Monday morning?"

"Good morning, Mr. Prime Minister. I'll come to the reason for my call in a moment. But first let me say that, while you and I haven't met, I've read a great deal about you. For a man who has just taken on the job — seven weeks I think it is now, isn't it?"

"That's right, Mr. President."

"Well, you seem to be getting things done, putting your team together, reorganizing policies and departments. We Texans like people who can move fast, and make decisions."

Suddenly the President's voice hardened. "Now, Mr. Prime Minister, let me tell you why I'm calling. As you're aware, I'm facing re-election next month. As a politician, you'll appreciate that I want to clean up as many loose ends as I can before the beginning of November so I can show the voters...."

"I understand, Mr. President."

"I thought you would. Well, what I want to talk to you about is natural gas. I should tell you at this point that I've discussed what I'm going to say with the leaders of the Senate and the House of Representatives, and with my Cabinet and my experts in the State Department. I have the full concurrence of all of them.

"Let me give you the background, Mr. Prime Minister. The United States is heading for another winter of disastrous shortages of natural gas. As you know, the energy crisis has been building up over the last decade. We've been able to offset it to a certain extent by increasing our imports of crude oil, but natural gas represents a far greater problem. Over 32% of the energy in this country is supplied by natural gas. We must have it if we are to survive. This year we expect a shortage of 2.7-trillion cubic feet. My advisers and the Federal Power Commission expect that in the area from Chicago and Detroit through to New York and Boston alone 20% of our industrial capacity will have to be shut down for the extremely cold parts of the winter. Apartment buildings and houses will be without heat; schools, hospitals and homes for the aged will have to be closed. In other words, Mr. Prime Minister, we are facing a national disaster.

"I recognize that there is absolutely nothing I can do in the short term to overcome this problem completely, but what I want to put to you is a long-term program that we can get working on right away."

Robert Porter leaned forward in his chair. "Mr. President, we're tremendously concerned about the problem up here. If there is any way Canada can help . . ."

The President cut him short. "That's just the trouble. For years now we've been trying to get you people to help, and all we get is a lot of talk. Now let me finish. I realize that you have most of the facts, but I want to get across

2

to you the position exactly as I see it.

"Our shortage of natural gas is caused largely by lack of transportation. While gas is produced in Algeria, the Middle East and Venezuela, there is no existing tanker fleet large enough to carry it to the United States. We've been trying desperately to build ships of our own. In late '72 we gave two contracts worth $569-million to General Dynamics and Newport News. We now have ten tankers in operation and ten more near completion, but that's only a drop in the bucket.

"Therefore, it's absolutely essential for us to obtain natural gas on the North American continent or in the Arctic Islands. And the gas is up there, all right. I'm told we can get 1½-trillion cubic feet a year out of Prudhoe Bay and the Mackenzie Delta by the Mackenzie Valley pipeline. The fact is, you have natural gas, and we're suffering because you've consistently refused to give us access and you've failed to plan intelligently. Look at the Mackenzie Valley pipeline. Almost all the financing has come from the United States, and we've worked with you people all the way to see that the economic impact of the construction would be good for Canada, and that the environmental boys would be kept happy. That pipeline is still being tested. It should be finished by now. I was counting on it being ready to start delivering gas next month. Now God knows when it will be completed. It must be at least six months behind schedule. And what's worse, because you didn't take our advice in dealing with the claims of the native peoples in the Northwest Territories, they started blowing up the pipeline ten days ago."

"Mr. President, you know the RCMP are investigating the bombings."

"Hell, you don't have a hope of finding anything. Those people can move in and blow up the pipe any place they like

3

and any time they like, and there's no way you can do a thing about it.

"For years we tried to convince Canada to follow our example and recognize aboriginal rights to a share of the natural wealth. When we settled with the people of Alaska in the early 70's we gave them $500-million, 40-million acres of land, and another $½-billion from a royalty of 2% on the oil and gas production from Prudhoe Bay.

"What did you people do? You got on your high horse and denied that the Indians and Eskimos had any claim to compensation, even though your government had signed treaties with some of the native groups in the Mackenzie Valley Corridor. I tell you, you have a moral obligation to them just as you have a moral obligation to see that the rest of us have natural gas so we can live and so our industries can keep going. But not one cubic foot of gas will flow in that pipeline until an agreement has been reached with the natives.

"Now, let's look at the Arctic Islands. Firms such as Imperial Oil, Tenneco, Columbia Natural Gas, and a host of others have poured more than $300-million into Panarctic's exploration program. The proved up gas reserves now total at least 60-trillion cubic feet. Melville Island is sitting on a bed of natural gas, and enormous finds have been made on King Christian, Ellef Ringnes, Thor, Axel Heiberg, Ellesmere, and other islands in the Sverdrup Basin. There's absolutely no doubt that by the time a transportation system is set up from the Islands to the mainland, the reserves will far exceed the 60-trillion mark. And virtually all the money for this exploration and development has come from the United States.

"The fact is, Prime Minister, Canada has the natural gas. The United States has paid for its discovery, and by

4

rights we own the stuff. We must have it, and must have it fast."

Porter interrupted. "Now just a minute. I realize you people have put money into the Arctic. So have we. We're prepared to make a deal to supply gas from the Islands on fair terms, but we have to protect...."

"Now, Prime Minister, you know that's not true. God knows we've been trying for years to get your government to come to grips with the situation. We've cajoled, wheedled, got on bended knee, and got absolutely nowhere. All we hear is the maddening response that Canada won't let us have any gas until its own needs for the future are determined and you see if there is any surplus you can afford to sell."

The President paused and cleared his throat. "Now let's get down to brass tacks. The United States can't put up with this situation any longer, and we're not going to. We must have three unconditional commitments from the Parliament of Canada, and we must have them by six o'clock tomorrow night.

"The first is that the aboriginal rights of the native people of the Yukon and the Northwest Territories will be recognized and that a settlement will be worked out with them at once along the lines of the Alaskan model.

"The second is that Canada will grant the United States full access to all the natural gas in the Arctic Islands without reference to Canada's future needs.

"And finally, I want a commitment that the United States will be allowed to create the transportation system necessary to move the gas as quickly as possible from the Arctic Islands to the United States. This commitment will have to include free access to the Islands across any Canadian territory which may provide a practical route.

5

"Now let me make this clear. I want these commitments by six o'clock tomorrow night, and they must be given by the Parliament of Canada, not simply the government. I know your Parliament isn't in session, but that's your problem, not mine."

The Prime Minister's eyes were wide with disbelief, and his voice betrayed his anger.

"Now hold on. If you think you can try to blackmail us into giving you people the right to take control of our resources, you'd better do some more thinking."

"Well, Mr. Prime Minister, it's up to you. I've given Canada an ultimatum. As you know, we have plenty of muscle to back it up — economic levers too numerous to list. I expect to hear from you by six o'clock tomorrow night. Good-bye."

The Prime Minister put the receiver down. His face was white with anger and astonishment. He reached for the intercom and punched the button for his chief executive assistant.

Tom Scott responded immediately. "Yes, sir."

"Tom, get in here fast, and alert your entire staff to stand by. We've got real trouble on our hands."

Scott burst into the office. The Prime Minister motioned for him to sit down.

"Tom, I've just had a telephone call from the President of the United States, and this is what he said. . . ."

When he had finished, all Scott could say was, "Good God! He must be crazy."

"No. He means business. He meant exactly what he said.

"Tom, get Mike and Tony in here. I want them to sit in a corner, take notes, and keep quiet. Also, I want your two best secretaries. Before you bring them in they must swear not to say a word to anybody about what is going on. They're going to have to know exactly what is in my mind up to a point, and I don't want any leaks. Nothing is to be said unless I authorize it.

"Also, have someone phone the cabinet ministers most closely concerned — that would be Energy, Northern Development, External Affairs, Defence, Environment, Transport and Finance. Ask them if they could be here with their deputies in twenty minutes. And advise the

Leader of the Opposition and the leaders of the other two parties that I would be obliged if they would meet with me on a matter of urgent national importance one hour from now, at 10:15. Tell each of them, Tom, that I have invited the others to attend, so they'll know they're not alone. I'll see the leaders here and the ministers in the Cabinet Room."

As Tom turned to go, he muttered, "Christ, he can't do this to us!"

The Prime Minister heard him. "Sure he can and he is. Furthermore, I can see why. I have enormous sympathy for him in the position he's in and for the thousands of Americans who are going to suffer this winter. But that doesn't make it any easier for us."

The Prime Minister turned to look out the window of his East Block office across Parliament Hill.

Robert Porter was new to the office of Prime Minister, but he had already established himself as a strong, forceful leader who had brought to his election campaign imaginative national goals with which almost all Canadians could personally identify. One of his main objectives was that the people of Canada should own all the crude oil and gas and all the exploration leasing rights for the natural resources in the Canadian Arctic. In Porter's view, the existing system under which foreign exploration firms were able to pick up drilling rights for between five and twenty cents an acre and pay royalties of only five to ten per cent on the well-head price when the oil and gas was finally found, left Canada with a "pittance" and put the ownership of control in foreign hands. Under Porter's program, control of the development in the Arctic would remain in Canadian hands, and the yearly revenue from

8

the sale of gas and oil from the Arctic Islands and the Mackenzie Delta, which could eventually range as high as $40-billion, would produce profits which could be used to reduce personal taxation and increase the standard of medical and other social services. Now it was clear that he was faced with a crisis which could threaten his whole program and require all his skills as a leader.

"Sir, we're ready."

It was Tom Scott, with his two young staff men and the secretaries.

The Prime Minister turned away from the window and repeated to the group what he had already told Scott, outlining the President's position.

"The reason I have brought you all in is this: I want to set out the course of action we must take within the next few hours so that a decision can be made on the ultimatum. Since you, Mike and Tony, will be working directly under Tom, I thought it was best that you should hear my instructions. Marie, I want you and Louise to take down what I say so that we'll have a record. I asked for both of you because, as you know, I sometimes speak rather quickly and I don't want to be interrupted. What I say will also be tape-recorded, so that you can double-check.

"Now Tom, there's no question in my mind that the House will have to be reconvened at once. The response to the ultimatum will have to come by a decision of Parliament on a free vote.

"One of the major problems is to make sure that every member of the House and the Senate is fully briefed on the state of Canada's relations with the United States and on the status of the oil and gas finds, as well as on the pipeline situation in the Mackenzie Valley Corridor. They must

9

also be filled in on the specifics of the current energy shortage in the U.S., and what has been happening since the early 70's.

"I want the premiers of each of the provinces informed as soon as possible, and I want them brought here to Ottawa immediately for consultation. When I decide on a course of action, I will have to clear with the Governor-General and also the Leader of the Opposition and the leaders of the other parties. I want their full concurrence and understanding so that we can work this thing out together."

Tom Scott nodded. "The party leaders will be here at 10:15, sir. The Governor-General is on his way back from Victoria. I'll leave word at Government House that you're to be informed immediately on his arrival."

"Good. I also want to meet with the leaders of the television and radio industry and the press, to see if I can get them to cool it. This situation will have to be handled carefully. I don't want anyone to panic.

"Tomorrow's agenda is even more important. It's the key to the whole thing. I have to get the decision to the President before six o'clock. The House and the Senate must meet and there has to be a reasonable time for debate. But the most important thing I have to do is to make sure that everyone understands the background of this whole situation.

"So here's what we're going to do. I want a briefing organized for eight o'clock tomorrow morning in the Commons Chamber. You can set that up with the Speaker, Tom.

"The briefing will be for all members of the House, the Senate, the premiers who can get here, and anyone else we think appropriate. It will be given by the ministers and deputy ministers of the departments which have an interest in the North and in oil and gas — Energy, Mines and Resources; Indian Affairs and Northern Development; Environment; Transport; External Affairs; Defence — also Finance. I want the lead-off to be External Affairs. The briefing must be over by eleven o'clock, because I want the House and the Senate to meet at twelve noon. As it is, that only gives us five hours for debate — less, actually, because the motion will have to be put before the House and I'll need half an hour at the end to close off. But we must be finished by five so that a vote can be taken in both houses before 5:30 and I can get back to the President with a decision by six.

"I'll ask the Leader of the Opposition and the other party leaders to help me draft the motion. I think that it should be put forward by all of us jointly."

Scott interjected, "Prime Minister, how in the hell are you going to sort out who's to speak during the debate, how long people are going to take and that sort of thing, so you can get through in time?"

"I don't see that as a real problem. The leaders are reasonable people, and I think the seriousness of the situation is such that we can set up a system that will be acceptable to all of them. Mind you, each of them is going to have to work out with his own people who is going to speak and for how long. That's one of the understandings I'll have to get from them when we meet, but I'm sure they'll cooperate.

"For now the major effort is to get Parliament reconvened and every member back here as fast as possible, wherever he is."

Porter turned to Mike Cranston. "Mike, I think you'd better get going. Phone the Chief of the Defence Staff immediately. Tell him to be prepared within an hour to divert all his Hercules transport aircraft to pick up members of

11

the House and the Senate who are at places off the main airline routes. We'll advise him as soon as possible where they'll have to go.

"Would you also tell the president, or the top man you can find at Air Canada, Canadian Pacific, and the regional carriers, that seats should be cleared for all members of Parliament, senators, and people whom we provide with special priority ratings. Also tell them that we may require special flights to be made off schedule.

"Then get on to the executive assistants of the leaders of the other parties so that they can communicate with their members to get back here. Tell them to let you know where their people are so that they can be picked up if they're off-route. And of course have someone get in touch with our own people."

As Mike Cranston headed for the door, the Prime Minister flicked the intercom switch for his secretary.

"Joan, would you please call and speak to the presidents of the National Press Gallery, the CBC, CTV, and Global Television. Ask them if they or their senior representatives can be at this office within an hour. Tell them I have an emergency on my hands that I must speak to them about and get their advice. Say they may have to wait, and I hope they won't mind. And find out exactly who will be coming."

"Yes, sir."

The Prime Minister turned back to Scott. "Tom, you'd better get on to the premiers now. I want them all here as quickly as possible. I guess the premiers from Ontario and Quebec won't need any help from us, but those from the West and the Maritimes may have to be given a hand getting here. That includes the Commissioners from the Northwest Territories and the Yukon, of course. I'd like you to make every effort to get them here by six tonight, because I want them involved in this decision."

Scott interjected, "What about the Cabinet, sir?"

"You're quite right, I've got to get the whole Cabinet together as soon as possible after I've met with the key ministers. I should be clear of the press by 12:15, so I'll call a Cabinet meeting for that time. Look after it, please.

"Now, one final thing. You've got a hell of a lot of work to do. We're going to have to schedule everything down to the minute. As we work toward the briefing at eight o'clock tomorrow morning, I don't want anyone to be talking to the press without my direct authority, and I want you to stay within shouting distance. Get in more staff if you need it."

Scott was already on his way to the door. He paused long enough to say, "I'll be here, sir. By the way, the press will be after you for a statement. What shall I tell them?"

"I don't see a press conference as being possible. Really, there isn't time. Anyway, I want to discuss that whole question with the news people when they're here."

When Scott and his assistants had left, Porter picked up the telephone and dialled a familiar number. In a moment he was through to John Thomas, a close and trusted friend whom he had appointed to the Senate.

"John, I've got real trouble. I've just had a call from the President of the United States. They're forecasting an even worse energy shortage this winter than our experts had predicted. On top of that he's really worried about the bombings along the Mackenzie pipeline. He's dropped a real crusher on us. By six o'clock tomorrow night we have to agree to settle with the native people and get the bombings stopped. We must also give him free access to the natural gas in the Arctic Islands and the right to set up a transportation system to get it out.

"You said once that if ever I needed your personal coun-

13

sel I was to let you know. Well, I need it now. I'd like you to drop everything and give me a hand until this whole thing is over with.

"I want you to sit in on all the meetings, listen and take notes. If something crosses your mind, scribble a message and pass it to me. I'm just going into the Cabinet Room now to meet my key ministers. If you could join me there as soon as possible I'd appreciate it."

"I'll be there in five minutes, Bob."

Sam Allen's eyes opened slowly as he wakened. Their dark brown pupils moved slightly from side to side as he focused on the white material of the tent just a few inches from his face. Then he remembered where he was.

His eyes closed again. They never opened very wide, for Sam Allen, like his Eskimo forefathers, had been raised on the land and the ice and the snow. The slitted eyes were those of the hunter who lived off the harvest of the sea and the animals which moved across the barren tundra.

But for young Sam, lying half asleep in his small white tent, pitched on the snow under a stand of jackpine next to the swath the gas pipeliners had made as they passed on their construction journey to the south two years before, life was not that of a hunter. In 1962 Sam's father, old Joe Allen, had moved, along with twelve other Eskimo trappers, from Tuktoyaktuk northeast across the ice to Sach's Harbour on Banks Island. There, it was said, white fox existed in abundance.

It was a good move. The white fox did indeed abound on Banks Island, and the white man paid good prices for the magnificent furs. The families at Sach's Harbour flourished and were prosperous. Sam's father had built a primitive but comfortable house for his wife and nine children. Sam, the oldest, went for his schooling to Inuvik with hundreds of other Eskimo and Indian children from the Mackenzie Delta region, brought there each fall to be educated according to the white man's plan. There they lived for nine months of the year, from the time each was the age of six until they finished high school, or decided, at the age of fifteen or sixteen, to drop out and stay with their families in the settlements or maybe get a job at Inuvik or with the pipeliners — or maybe not work at all.

Sam Allen had lived through that cruel process of education which the white man had decided was best for the Indian and Eskimo. He had survived the wrench of being taken from his family at such a young age to live under the benign regimentation of the Anglican priests who ran the hostel to which he was assigned. As Sam grew older, his education increased far beyond that of his father, Joe Allen, and it became much more difficult for Sam and his classmates to return home at the close of the school year to their families living in tents or shacks in the settlements all along the Arctic coast.

Sam Allen had indeed survived the educational system. He was a determined, headstrong, intelligent, inventive young man. Unusually proficient in mathematics, he had been encouraged to go south to the University of Alberta at Edmonton to take a degree in civil engineering. His tuition and expenses were paid for by the government of the Northwest Territories. Sam worked hard, and graduated near the top of his class. Long before he finished at the university, he had been approached by several of the major oil companies who all wanted the first Eskimo ever to graduate as an engineer. He would be very valuable to the company which got him as a symbol that they were co-operating with the Eskimo people. Sam listened carefully to each of the proposals, thanked each of the company representatives, and said he would be in touch before the end of his final year. Then he kept on with his studies.

It had been 1970 when Sam, still a teenager, had become

deeply involved in the work of COPE, the Committee for Original People's Entitlement. The government, without any consultation with the Eskimo trappers who occupied Banks Island, had granted rights to a French company to drill exploration wells and do seismic tests. When the oil exploration people arrived with their first equipment, all hell broke loose. COPE became immediately involved in an attempt to protect the Sach's Harbour Eskimos. They retained a Yellowknife lawyer and eventually, after the threat of an injunction, an agreement was worked out between the government and the local people. Even then it was apparent to Sam that the main intention of the government departments was not to protect the native people but to push for exploration and development. This meant that the native people had to organize to protect themselves. So Sam had become involved in the work of COPE while he was still at school in Inuvik, and was soon recognized as a born leader. At Inuvik, too, he had met the new lawyer who had come to practise there, Robert Porter. Porter had taken an interest in Sam, and it was he who had encouraged him to go on to university.

Now Robert Porter was Prime Minister, and Sam Allen a graduate civil engineer working with Imperial Oil in the Mackenzie Delta, leader of COPE, and a militant spokesman for the native people. Although Robert Porter had made a full commitment to recognize the aboriginal rights of the Eskimos and Indians of the Northwest Territories and the Yukon and to provide a settlement similar to that made by the United States with the Alaskan native people, negotiations had not yet got under way. The native people, even Sam Allen, felt that Porter ought to move more quickly, because the pipeline was now almost finished. After three years, the southern section from the United States border near Killdeer, Saskatchewan, north to

17

Yellowknife was complete. The last sections near Camsell Bend, northwest of Yellowknife, were under construction, linking Yellowknife to Prudhoe Bay and the Mackenzie Delta. But no settlement had been made with the native people. When the construction jobs were gone, nothing would be left. The Indians and Eskimos would be as poor as before, while the white man drained away their natural wealth. Something had to be done. Sam Allen was doing it.

Sam turned over on his right side to look into the sleeping face of his woman. Bessie Tobac was a Loucheux Indian girl whom he had known from the time they were both at school in Inuvik. She was three years younger than Sam, and he had not paid much attention to her then. But when he arrived back from university and had started to work for COPE, he found that Bessie was already a vice-president of the organization. She had been working at the craft shop at Inuvik for about five years, and had become the first native person to be promoted to be assistant manager of that store. Like Sam, she was bright, and totally dedicated to the cause of her people.

As Sam looked at her still sleeping, he could see wisps of her raven black hair sticking out from under the parka hood which framed her somewhat angular face, thin nose and full red lips. He gently put his arm around her and moved his bare left leg to wedge it between Bessie's, and forced them gently apart. At his touch, Bessie's eyes opened to look into Sam's. She smiled at him and put her arm around him, and her legs opened in response to his pressure. It was time to make love. It was time to begin the day.

In the hours ahead they would finish laying the last of the ten packages of high explosive they had brought with them out of Inuvik the day before.

The Prime Minister entered the Cabinet Room. After greetings were exchanged and everyone was seated, he said, "Gentlemen, I have brought you here to advise me. We are facing an emergency of the first magnitude. Since you represent the ministries most closely involved in the crisis, I felt that I should consult with you first."

He then went on to report the telephone call from the President and the nature of the ultimatum from the United States. When he was finished, his audience was shocked and incredulous.

Without pausing for comment, the Prime Minister continued quickly, "We will, of course, discuss the situation in detail at the full Cabinet meeting later today. Now I want you to prepare for a briefing to be held tomorrow morning at eight o'clock.

"The briefing will be for all members of Parliament, including the Senate, and the provincial premiers who can get here. It should be a crash course for everyone on the status of the Arctic Islands gas and oil discoveries and development. For example, it should cover the number of rigs in operation there, the number of people involved, the ownership and control of the gas and oil fields, the interests of Panarctic, and the position of Tenneco, Columbia Gas, and other major American firms that have been advancing money to Panarctic for exploration work. It should deal with the estimated reserves of natural gas and oil and the commitments made by Panarctic and the other owners in the islands to United States firms. And it should also give the National Energy Board's figures on what they calculate will be surplus to Canada's requirements.

"Then I want the same information for the Mackenzie Delta region, and I want growth and demand figures for the United States itself, an analysis of their energy crisis and of the long-term efforts they've taken to cope with it.

"The next thing we'll need is a status report on the Mackenzie Valley pipeline, the problems that have occurred, both in building it and financing it. We should also be brought up to date on the state of the government's discussions with the native people concerning aboriginal rights, and on the sabotage which has been taking place.

"Then I would like to have an informed guess on the type and scope of the economic sanctions that the United States might impose if we refuse to give in to their ultimatum, and a review of the sanctions and other measures they've used in the past two decades to protect their economy and world trading position.

"A similar survey showing what forms of military pressure have been invoked by the United States in various parts of the world since 1945 would be useful. External and National Defence could work that out for us.

"Finally we should have a review of the United States' position concerning our sovereignty in the Arctic, dating back to the *Manhattan* voyages in 1969 and '70, and the enactment of the Arctic Waters Pollution Prevention Act at that time.

"The objective I have in mind, gentlemen, is to give every member of the House a factual briefing on the background behind each element of the ultimatum. I think you'll be surprised at how little most members know about what is going on in the Canadian Arctic about oil and gas, and about our ongoing relationship with the United States and with our native people.

"The briefing will be in the Commons Chamber. As I said, it will start at 8 a.m. Each of you will have twenty-five minutes to make your presentation and answer questions. That's really very little time, but it's the best we can do under the circumstances. I want the briefings to be precise and to the point. They must be finished by eleven o'clock because the House will sit at twelve noon to debate the ultimatum. I have no objection if a deputy minister rather than the minister makes the presentation, and of course you can be assisted by any other advisers you wish."

At this point, Tom Scott entered the room and spoke quietly to the Prime Minister. After receiving instructions, he nodded and departed. The Prime Minister turned back to his colleagues.

"Mr. Scott has just informed me that the office of the President has been on the line. He requests permission to make a flight over Canadian territory to inspect the Polar Gas Study experimental station on Melville Island and to inform himself of conditions in the North generally. I can see nothing to be gained by refusing this permission. Indeed, we may gain by granting it. The President may have more understanding when he sees the difficulties under which we've been operating. I've therefore told Tom to give the President clearance. I trust this meets with your approval."

There was a general murmur of consent, and the Prime Minister continued. "Now to get back to the briefing session: Bob, I want you to start off."

The Prime Minister was speaking to Robert Gendron, Minister for External Affairs. Gendron was the Prime

Minister's right-hand man in the Cabinet, the leader of the Quebec sector of the party, and by far the most experienced of all the ministers.

"I think it's important for you to give a broad overview of our relationship with the United States. I don't care who follows after that. It might be a good idea if you carried on with this meeting now to sort out the details. There is to be a full Cabinet meeting at 12:15, so as soon as you can get your staffs going on the briefing material the better.

"I have asked for a meeting with the Leader of the Opposition and the other parties. They should be waiting for me now. I hope you will excuse me."

Sam Allen bent over to strap on his second snowshoe. As he did so he said to Bessie, "We've got a tough day ahead of us. I've planned to set these last five charges along a fifteen-mile stretch. We're going to have to hurry to finish and meet Freddie at Rat Lake at six." He straightened up and looked southwest down the 120-foot swath cut by the pipeliners to where the pipe emerged at the river's edge. Although the pipe had not been buried completely in the permafrost and tundra, it had been sunk halfway down, and the part above the surface covered over with a mound of earth or "berm" of gravel and soil so that the natural vegetation could grow and cover over the pipe. In this way it was hoped the wildlife would not be impeded and that the whole corridor could return to an apparent state of nature. Because of the covering, Sam had had to set the charges at water-crossings. He knew there was no natural gas in the pipe yet but that it was under pressure for testing, and that the moment the first explosion went off, the company would get reconnaissance helicopters out to locate the break and find any other explosives which they had set. This was what had happened when the first set of five bombs had blown the pipe successfully two weeks before.

Sam and Bessie slipped their heads through the holes in the white sheets which they had brought to provide some camouflage against a possible survey helicopter patrolling the line. Bessie said, "I'm ready to go. Shall we leave the tent and packs here, Allen, while we set this charge?"

"I think so." Sam reached into the small tent and dragged out an old and much-used knapsack. From inside he carefully drew out a small blue plastic bag. The package was about the size and weight of a 32-ounce bottle of booze. But, as Sam had said to Bessie, it packed one hell of a lot more wallop. The plastic explosives were powerful enough to rip out a five-foot section of 48-inch steel pipe cleanly. Attached to the explosive was an arming device and a timer mechanism, both of which had to be delicately engaged once the bomb was in place.

With the timer, Sam had planned to set the bombs to go off at random intervals down the line over a twelve-day period. Although this bomb was the sixth to be placed, it actually would explode two days later.

The arming mechanism had a fail-safe device designed to prevent anyone from disarming the bomb once the charge was in place and the timer set. Projecting through the casing of the unit was the rim of a small wheel. To disarm the bomb, the wheel had to be turned fully clockwise and the connecting wires removed between the explosive and the timer. If the wheel were turned counter-clockwise it would detonate the explosive charge and, with it, the person turning the wheel.

When they reached the pipe, Sam handed the explosives to Bessie and, taking the shovel, chopped away at the snow around the base of the pipe where it re-entered the berm. Then he laid the plastic bag out on the snow between his snowshoes, squatted down on his haunches, and set out the arming device, timer and plastics in front of him. He connected the two wires running from the plastic charge through the detonator to the timing unit and pulled back his sleeve to check the time. It was 7:50. He reached inside his pocket to fish out the piece of paper on which he had marked the locations of the ten bombs, together with the date and times selected for their explosion. The list confirmed a time of eleven o'clock two days from now.

He set the timer for 51 hours, and then wrote down on the list the number and date of the bomb, the time at which it was planted, and the time delay. He set the marker on the disarm wheel and pushed in the red arming button. He could feel it engage. The bomb was armed, the timer was set.

He turned to Bessie and nodded. At the signal she stooped over and gingerly lifted the explosive package while Sam picked up the arming device and timer. They lowered the bomb back into the plastic bag. Then Sam eased it into the opening he had made in the snow and covered it over, smoothing out the surface.

"That's it," he said. "Let's pick up the stuff and move on."

As they turned to go back to the tent, they suddenly stopped. In the distance there was a faint chopping sound. Bessie shouted, "Helicopter!"

In their clumsy snowshoes they raced for the edge of the clearing and the protection of the trees. They knew from the sound that the helicopter was very close and flying low. They threw themselves in the snow between the trees and pulled the white sheets up over their heads, covering themselves completely, except for their snowshoes. As they lay in the snow barely daring to breathe, Sam could hear the blades of the helicopter whacking through the air just above the treeline as it passed straight over top of them. He knew that the pilot and the observer in the helicopter had probably been airborne for at least two hours out of the Canadian Arctic gas base near Arctic Red River. By this time, their eyes would be tired from the

25

bright sunlight and they probably wouldn't be able to see very much, even the snowshoe tracks. Sam was right. The helicopter went straight on, without pausing.

When they were certain that the helicopter was gone, Sam and Bessie got up, went quickly back to the tent, packed up, and then set off at a fast pace down the pipeline corridor.

When the Prime Minister returned to his office following his meeting with the key cabinet ministers, he found the leaders of the opposition parties waiting for him.

The Leader of the Opposition, George Foot, a man whom Porter respected, greeted the Prime Minister warmly as they shook hands. So did Donald Walker, the Leader of the New Democratic Party, and Pierre Johnson, of the Social Credit. All three men had been in the House of Commons for many years — a good deal longer than the Prime Minister — and they let him know it from time to time during the heat of debate. But though he was much younger than any one of them, they clearly recognized his ability.

As the Prime Minister was about to explain the urgent reason for the meeting, John Thomas entered the office. Porter introduced him. "Gentlemen, this is Senator Thomas. I don't think any of you have met him personally, but I'm sure you all know who he is. He is not only my close friend, but my personal counsel as well. I've asked him to sit in on all my meetings during the next few hours. I hope you don't mind if he joins us. When I get through explaining what is going on, I think you will understand why I need his presence."

Without waiting for reply, the Prime Minister went straight on. "At nine o'clock this morning I received a telephone call from the President of the United States. As you are all aware, the United States faces an unparalleled energy shortage this coming winter, most particularly a shortage of natural gas. The President, facing re-election next month, has given me an ultimatum which has to be answered unconditionally by Parliament by tomorrow night at six o'clock."

The Prime Minister quickly outlined the three conditions of the ultimatum. When he had finished, George Foot exclaimed, "Why, that's straight blackmail!"

All three opposition leaders were clearly appalled by what they had heard. Johnson stuttered, "Did he say what the United States would do if Canada refused to give in?"

"No," the Prime Minister replied. "I asked him, but all he would say was that he had economic levers too numerous to list. I can think of two or three right off the top. I will be instructing the President of the Treasury Board and the Governor of the Bank of Canada to get their staffs going on estimating the kind of sanctions they think the President can impose, and the probable effect, but just for openers the Americans could levy a prohibitive tax on all manufactured goods coming from Canada. They could prohibit American investors from buying Canadian securities, or in any other way investing money in Canada. By itself, that sanction would practically destroy the Canadian economy, because we need the inflow of U.S. and other foreign capital in order to stay alive."

The Leader of the Opposition agreed. "No question about it. And I suppose they could even stop taking our natural resources, except of course the commodities which they desperately need in their energy crisis, the gas and oil."

It was Pierre Johnson's turn. "They could even go so far as to cut off our shipping or prevent goods from crossing the border. But they would never do that, do you think? We've been on the best of terms with the Americans always. I can't conceive of their doing such things."

"I can," said the Prime Minister. "And I can also see why they're taking this course of action. What we must discuss now are the steps we can take to handle this situation.

"First, I hope we can agree to put aside party considerations. I do not expect you to give up your right to quarrel with anything I do or say, but at this moment bear in mind that what I need is your advice and counsel, not criticism."

George Foot immediately responded, "Prime Minister, there are many differences between us and there always will be, but in this situation my party will do its utmost to co-operate with the government." Johnson and Walker made similar announcements, much to the relief of the Prime Minister.

"Thank you, gentlemen, I hoped you would agree. Now, to get down to business. I think it is obvious that Parliament must be recalled. I have already issued instructions that this step be taken and that emergency transportation be arranged under the direction of the Chief of the Defence Staff. I want every member of the House and Senate here in time for a briefing in the Commons at eight o'clock tomorrow morning. Following the briefing, which will provide information for the members on all matters relevant to Arctic development and the current energy crisis in the United States, the House should convene in emergency session at twelve noon. The Senate can sit at the same time, and I will ask the Government Leader of the Senate to make sure that the motion which is debated is exactly the same as the one the House considers and that no vote is taken by the Senate until the House has voted.

"We must conclude debate by five o'clock, so the vote can be completed by 5:15 to allow the Senate to vote by

29

5:30. I propose that the vote in the House be a free vote so that no one is tied to party lines."

All three party leaders nodded their agreement.

"Good. The ideal thing would be for the four of us to prepare a motion and present it jointly to the House. The way we put it forward should be no indication whatsoever of the way in which any one of us is going to vote on the question. In introducing the motion I'll make that perfectly clear."

The Prime Minister was interrupted as Tom Scott quietly entered the room and handed him a note. Porter read it, whispered briefly to Scott, then carried on.

"If we open the House at twelve noon and commence the vote at five o'clock, that leaves just five hours for debate; actually, somewhat less than that, because I would like to have thirty minutes at the end to sum up and ten minutes at the beginning to get the ball rolling. Obviously we are going to have to control the number of speakers and the time for debate very rigidly. I would suggest that each of you take fifteen minutes and that all other speakers be limited to ten."

Pierre Johnson broke in. "Good heavens, Prime Minister, in fifteen minutes I can't even get started!"

His colleagues all laughed. Johnson was a notoriously long-winded though colourful speaker.

"Sorry, Pierre, this is one time when your eloquence will have to be contained."

None of the other leaders had any objection to the proposal. The Prime Minister continued.

"I also suggest that the number of speakers from each party be in proportion to the seats in the House. If we four take a total of fifty-five minutes for our remarks, that brings us to 12:55. Between 12:55 and 4:30 there are 215 minutes. At ten minutes per speaker, that works out to twenty-one speakers, more or less. Based on the present proportion in the House, that should give us ten speakers from the government, six from the Opposition, three from the NDP and two from Social Credit.

"For myself, I would open the debate by putting forward the motion in our joint names, and take that opportunity to provide the House with the background of the President's telephone call. Although this will have been extensively covered at the eight o'clock briefing, I think it should be repeated for Hansard."

"That's fine as far as my party is concerned, Prime Minister," said George Foot. "But we would very much appreciate knowing something about the line which you are going to take at the opening. If you could let us have a brief sketch of your remarks, it would be helpful. We will then be in a position to prepare our speeches so they will not cut across your approach or be contradictory. If I *have* to take a position on any point which is contrary to what you say in your remarks, that would also give me the opportunity of letting you know before the debate starts.

"Let me put it to you another way. I'm personally most anxious that all of us in the House present a solid front to the Americans and to our own public, as far as possible, but at this moment I don't know what the motion is going to be and I don't know all the facts. So I can't tell you now, Bob, what the final position of my party is going to be, or, for that matter, since it is a free vote, what my own position is going to be. However, as a matter of principle, I do feel very strongly that if Parliament can come out of this with a unanimous decision, or one which is close to it, it will strengthen Canada's position in negotiating with the representatives of the United States in the future. To have Parliament split in a crisis of this magnitude would be a disaster."

31

"I certainly agree, George. What do you think, Donald?"

Donald Walker had been the Leader of the NDP for many years. He had led his party in opposition to the building of the Mackenzie Valley gas pipeline and the sale of Arctic natural gas and oil to the United States. Furthermore, he had encouraged his party to take a position of strong economic nationalism, and he frequently made heavy attacks on corporations under foreign control. For Donald Walker, this moment of confrontation with the United States was an event which he had long and eagerly anticipated. His grey, sallow face, topped by a thatch of white hair, reflected little emotion, however, when he said, "Prime Minister, you and all of Canada know fully the position which my party has historically taken against the export of natural gas to the United States and against the building of the Mackenzie Valley pipeline. We have long expected that the American corporations, and the U.S. government, having failed completely to plan for their country's future energy requirements, and having taken no steps toward controlling their escalating population, would inevitably take such a step. The New Democratic Party has few members in the House, but our voice is strong. I can tell you one thing, and that is that I will do my best to persuade my party to stand against this intolerable American threat regardless of the consequences.

"So far as I am concerned, the proposals for the briefing tomorrow morning and the handling and timing of the debate are satisfactory. Subject only to seeing the form of the motion you propose, I will be pleased to move it jointly with the three of you."

The Prime Minister smiled and nodded. "Thank you, Donald. Your position is one which has not come as a complete surprise to me. Your willingness to co-operate is much appreciated.

"Now, Pierre, how about you?"

Pierre Johnson cleared his throat. "Prime Minister, so far as the arrangements are concerned, they sound fine to me. I am not going to say what my position will be until the debate. I want my own members to make up their own minds, since it is to be a free vote. I do feel that this is no time for Canadians to cling to regional or cultural differences, and I offer you my co-operation and my support."

"Thank you, Pierre.

"Well, gentlemen, I won't keep you any longer. I will try to keep you informed as matters develop, and to consult with you as the circumstances require. I have also asked the provincial premiers to be in Ottawa by six o'clock tonight. I feel that their views should be solicited and that they should take part in the decision-making process over the next few hours. I hope this meets with your approval."

The other party leaders nodded their heads in assent.

"One final thing," said the Prime Minister. "I've asked the President of the National Press Gallery, and the networks, or their senior representatives, to meet with me. Tom Scott has just informed me they are here. I'm going to ask them to play down as much as possible the ultimatum given to us by the President. The last thing I want is for the country to panic, so we'll need maximum restraint from the media."

As the opposition leaders rose to go, George Foot said, "Well, I wish you luck, Prime Minister. You'll do well to keep the press under control with a news story as big as this one. But you can rest assured that I and my party will do nothing to make this situation more difficult. If we stand together we will show the President that we have some muscle too."

The President loped across the green lawn of the White House toward the huge Navy helicopter waiting for him, its blades already starting to turn.

A tall, angular, athletic man, he moved quickly and decisively. His white hair blew wildly in the down-draught from the idling blades as he entered the door, followed by a retinue of six aides and secret service agents, all lugging their briefcases and green army-issue parkas, a strange sight on a warm autumn morning in Washington.

The President acknowledged the salute of the chief crewman as he entered the aircraft. He shoved his mane of hair back in place. As he walked toward the cockpit of the monster helicopter, he stripped off his coat and threw it on one of the passenger seats. Without breaking stride, he ducked his head as he entered the cockpit.

"Are we all set to go, Mac?"

The pilot replied, "Yes, we are, Mr. President. I've got all the taps on, and we've got traffic clearance across to Dulles at 3,000 feet."

"O.K., let's go. I'll ride as a passenger on this one."

Flying the helicopter, flying Air Force One, flying anything he could get his hands on was an enormous release for the President. He had been a pilot, and a first-class one, from the time he was twenty, when he joined the USAF. He had become one of their top fighter pilots in the European theatre, flying P51's in the Eighth Air Force as escort for the B17 Flying Fortresses. During his tour of operations he had shot down eight enemy aircraft and eventually had commanded his own squadron. There were times when, after long escort flights of six or seven hours, the ground crew would have to lift him out of the airplane. He would be so stiff from being cramped into the small cockpit that he couldn't move.

After the war, when he had graduated from law school and started to practise law in Houston, he kept up his flying. He had also begun to take part in his family's oil business, and the firm's fleet of aircraft provided him with an opportunity to maintain his standards. Even now, at the age of fifty-nine, the President of the United States flew as often as he could.

After the short hop from the White House lawn to Dulles, the helicopter set down with a bit of a bump about fifty yards away from the enormous silver Boeing 747, Air Force One, which was sitting waiting for him on the ramp. He and his six companions immediately transferred to the giant aircraft to join the large staff already on board. The President went directly to the cockpit.

The captain of the 747, Colonel Mike Wypich, with whom the President had flown so many times, had Air Force One set up for him in the usual way and was just completing the pre-flight checks. Finally Wypich said, "It's all yours, sir."

The President responded, "Good." Then he changed his mind. "No, you taxi out, Mike. I need practice in taking down the clearance."

He called Dulles Ground Control for taxi clearance, then switched to Departure Control for flight clearance. Both came through immediately. The President's pen moved rapidly as he copied down the details on his route pad. When the controller had finished reading the message to him, the President read it back to confirm that he had it correct. "ATC clears Air Force One to the Resolute Bay airport via direct Westminster, Jet 75 Plattsburgh, high level 567 Montreal, high level 570 Chibougamau, high level 572 Poste de la Baleine, INS direct Resolute, to maintain flight level 410. Depart Runway One right. After take-off maintain runway heading for radar vectors."

The voice of the Air Controller came back. "Your clearance checks. Go to Dulles tower frequency now." Then, in a rare lapse of procedure, the controller said to one of his buddies, "Hey that sounds like the man himself!" The President chuckled as he dialled up Dulles tower on the radio and took control from Mike Wypich.

At 10:32 Eastern Daylight Saving Time, the President got the huge 747 smoothly off the ground, rotating to pick it up cleanly at 160 knots. He climbed away on runway heading in accordance with his clearance.

The captain raised the landing gear on signal and changed over to departure frequency, contacted Departure Control, and received instructions to turn left to a heading of 350 degrees for vectors to the Westminster VOR. The President started a gentle left turn, and after rolling the 747 out on the assigned heading, asked for the after-take-off checks.

The route Air Force One was to follow today would take it over Albany and Plattsburgh, and then on northward over Canadian air space to Montreal's St. Eustache VOR, Chibougamau, Poste de la Baleine on the south-east coast of Hudson Bay, and then across Hudson Bay and the Boothia Peninsula on a course directly to Resolute Bay, on the 747's Inertial Navigation System.

When the aircraft reached its assigned flight altitude, the captain and engineer settled it to cruise at 480 knots. At that point the President said, "Give me your ETA for

Montreal, Mike, so that I can report as we pass over Albany VOR. When I've done that she's all yours. I've got to get back and get to work again."

The Albany VOR station was Air Force One's first check-point where, by international flight rules, they were obliged to report to the air traffic control people their position, altitude, and their estimated time of arrival (ETA) at the next check-point.

The captain responded immediately, "ETA over Montreal is 11:35, sir."

"Check."

As the big aircraft sliced through the clear air on course and at designated altitude, the President checked his flight director instruments and his radio magnetic indicator needles. Their VOR receivers were tuned in to a frequency of 117.8 MHz, and as the aircraft passed over Albany the RMI needles moved from pointing towards the nose of the aircraft through 180 degrees until they pointed to the tail. Observing this station passage, the President pressed his transmitter switch and spoke into the microphone. "Boston Centre, this is Air Force One. Over."

The reply was instantaneous. "Air Force One, this is Boston Centre. Go."

"Air Force One is by Albany at 11:08, flight level 410 IFR, estimating Montreal at 11:35 en route to Resolute Bay."

"Roger. Air Force One, we read two fast-moving aircraft your altitude at this time, moving your direction on intercept course about 50 miles from you at one o'clock position."

"Roger," the President replied. He turned to the captain. "You get that, Mike?"

"Yes, sir, I sure did. We'll keep an eye open."

"O.K.," the President said. "You have control. I'm going

to go back to my paperwork. I have to address the nation from this old bird at 12:30, and I've got to find out what my staff want me to say. You know how much us Texans like to be told what to say." The President's long angular face broke into a grin.

The captain laughed. "I sure do, Mr. President."

With that the President took off his head-set, unstrapped it, and left the cockpit.

As the three party leaders left his office, the Prime Minister motioned to Senator Thomas to stay. He went back to his desk, pushed the intercom button for his secretary, and asked, "Have you any messages I should know about?"

"No, Prime Minister, but I can tell you that Mr. Scott has been on the phone constantly, with people calling and trying to find out what's been going on."

"I'll bet he has. Tell me the names of the people who've turned up from the press."

"Peter Forbes, President of the National Press Gallery is here. You know him, Prime Minister. And the Executive Vice-President of the CBC, James Laing, came. He's agreed also to represent CTV and Global, so there are just these two gentlemen."

"Would you ask them to come in, please."

The Prime Minister turned to Senator Thomas. "We can have a few words when these people leave, John."

From the chair in the corner of the room which was to be his listening post, Thomas replied, with a wry smile, "Bob, I wouldn't miss this for the world."

The Prime Minister moved toward the main entrance door to greet Forbes and Laing as they entered the office.

"Peter, good to see you, and you, Jim. Have you people met Senator John Thomas? I've asked Senator Thomas to sit in on all the meetings I will be having in the next few hours so he can assist me in keeping some balance and perspective as well as give me advice."

When they were seated, the Prime Minister gave them a rapid-fire rundown on the President's ultimatum, the action he had already taken, and the plans to recall Parliament, bring in the premiers, carry out the major briefing the next morning, and convene the House and Senate during the afternoon.

Peter Forbes was almost beside himself with excitement. When the Prime Minister completed his explanation of the situation, Forbes practically shouted, "This is a fantastic story. Good God, I've got to get to my paper fast!" He looked around the room as if he were trying to figure out the quickest exit.

"Now wait a minute, Peter," Porter said calmly. "That's the real reason I want to talk with you and Jim. This might be the story of your lifetime, but it's also the worst and most disastrous crisis this country has had to face outside wartime. You people are in highly responsible positions, and you'll be among the first to recognize that if this story goes rocketing off, there could well be panic across Canada. I don't want that to happen, and I'm sure you don't either. So what I want to talk to you about is how the press can help control the situation."

James Laing put in cautiously, "What do you have in mind, sir?"

"I guess what I have in mind is something that really can't be done." The Prime Minister turned away from the two men facing him and looked out the window as he thought the question over. "What I really would like to see is a conscious effort by the press, TV and radio people to play this situation down. I don't want the newspapers to have four-inch headlines saying, 'Crisis Canada' or 'U.S. Ultimatum.' I don't want the television and radio programs to be interrupted with emergency bulletins. I would like to see a sort of normal, everyday reporting of the U.S. proposals and how we are dealing with them, just as if we had a routine situation on our hands. I'm not suggesting for one moment that the facts be suppressed or that the news be controlled. My concern is that the people of Canada should not be panicked."

Forbes, a peppery, excitable little fellow, the senior Ottawa Hill reporter with one of the Montreal papers, took the stance Porter had expected. In a rather hostile voice he said, "Are you suggesting, sir, that the press in this country are irresponsible or that we would deliberately go out of our way to over-emphasize the importance of this story just to sell newspapers? The press has always treated you fairly, Prime Minister, and I don't see why you think...."

The Prime Minister broke in. "I'm not making any such suggestion, Peter, but what I do recognize is that there are human beings running the newspapers and the news-rooms and television stations across this country. How they react to this whole situation will largely dictate how they will print the story.

"Let me lay the thing right on the table for you. I am very much afraid that there will be a strong and possibly violent anti-American reaction among the people of Canada, especially among those who live close to the American border. The last thing I want is to see the people of this country worked up to such a state that some foolish acts of reprisal will be taken against American citizens in Canada by wild-eyed nationalistic Canadians whose emotional juices are turned on, not only by the ultimatum itself, but by inflammatory reporting."

Laing raised a calming hand toward Peter Forbes and said to the Prime Minister, "I see your point, sir. What you say about reaction by the Canadian people is probably quite true. The last thing in the world I would want to see would be some act of violence against American nationals. That would set up a valid reason in the President's mind for some sort of reprisal, perhaps even military action, against Canada. Maybe that's just what he'd like to see at this time, and it's exactly the sort of thing that might happen, not only between now and tomorrow night but for some time after that." Laing hesitated. "But the problem is, sir, that I don't know what can be done about it."

"I agree, Prime Minister," said Forbes. "But how can I, or anyone in the Press Gallery, for that matter, convince his editor to play it cool? Frankly, sir, I don't think there's a hope in hell that you can keep the lid on this."

Senator John Thomas' voice rumbled from the corner, startling all three of them. "Prime Minister, I wonder if you might permit me to put in a word."

"Sure, John, please do."

"Well, it seems to me that there's only one person in Canada who can explain the situation to the people and make them see matters in the proper light, and that's you.

"I suggest that rather than place the burden upon Mr. Laing and Mr. Forbes or their colleagues, you take the matter before the whole country. I think you should appear on national television some time later today and make a statement to the nation. You should outline the seriousness of the situation and directly suggest to the press, radio and TV people that every effort should be made to keep all the facts in perspective, that the American position in the energy crisis should be understood, and that typical Canadian calmness and coolness should prevail."

Laing nodded his head in agreement. "I think that's an excellent idea, Prime Minister. The CBC will clear its national TV network for you at any time, and I know CTV and Global will do the same. In fact, I would be pleased to speak to them for you if you wish."

The Prime Minister turned to Forbes. "What do you think, Peter?"

"Sounds good to me, sir, but I suggest that you get something out to the public as quickly as possible."

"All right, then. I'll need some time to prepare a statement. What about nine o'clock this evening? Could you clear half an hour at that time for me, Jim?"

Laing replied, "No problem, sir, but is there any possibility of your doing it earlier?"

"I don't think so. There's just too much to be done. However, I think I can put together a press release, although there isn't time for a press conference now. You can alert your people that a release will be made in half an hour. In the meantime, I'd like both of you to keep this discussion in confidence, and, Jim, if you will check with CTV and Global and clear the network time with them as well, I'd appreciate it. Would you get in touch with Tom Scott, my chief executive assistant, when the matter has been arranged? Also would you let him know if there are any snags? I think it would be appropriate to carry the program on your radio network as well."

As the Prime Minister stood up to terminate the meeting, there was a quick knock on the door, and Tom Scott entered.

"Sir, we've just had word that the President is going on television at 12:30. It looks as though he's going to make a public announcement about the ultimatum."

Porter was silent for a moment or two. Then he turned to Laing and Forbes and said, "Well, gentlemen, it looks as though the time-table is now somewhat out of our hands. Jim, I would appreciate it if you could clear your television network for me to speak immediately after the President's address. I'll try to deal with the points he raises at that time and make it as short as I can. In any event, I will still want to do the lengthy and considered statement at nine o'clock. Can you arrange it?"

Laing looked at his watch and exclaimed, "My God, it's now two minutes to twelve. We've just a little over half an hour. If you can let me use the phone I think we can arrange for you to follow the President, but we'll have to hustle. As far as nine o'clock tonight is concerned, that's no problem. I'll get onto our technical people immediately to get a TV camera and crew up here. I understand you have a cable and hookup for transmission in the Conference Room down the hall."

Tom Scott said, "That's right."

"Good. We'll use that room for your broadcast. Now, Mr. Scott, if you can get me to a telephone I'll get everything set up."

After getting Laing started on his calls, Scott returned to the Prime Minister's office and reported, "Sir, all the members of the Cabinet are now in the Cabinet Room. I've also arranged for the six deputy ministers of the key departments and the Governor of the Bank of Canada to be present."

Porter nodded. "Good. You'd better get the Deputy Minister of National Defence, too, if he's available. How are the arrangements for transportation coming?"

"Very well, sir. Things seem to be going smoothly. Also the premiers are on their way now."

"That's fine. Now if you'll look after Mr. Forbes, I want to have a brief word with Senator Thomas before I meet the Cabinet. "Thanks again, Peter. I appreciate your advice and co-operation."

As the door shut behind them, Porter said, "Well, John, what do you think of the situation?" He walked over to a massive easy chair in front of the great stone fireplace, lowered himself into it, and put his feet up on the coffee table.

Thomas sat down opposite him, put his notebook and pen on the table, and said, "I think you've got all the bases covered, Bob. While you're dealing with the Cabinet, do you want me to put together the draft press release? You remember you told Forbes you'd have one in half an hour."

"I forgot about that when I heard the President was going to speak. No, it won't be necessary now that I'm going on TV. My shot at that time will be more than sufficient, so don't waste your time putting anything together."

Thomas nodded. "Right. Now the only other question I have is this. Do you think there's any possibility of getting the President to extend his time limit? It seems to me that after all these years of negotiating and haggling another day or two shouldn't matter much to him. But it would give you and the whole country a far better opportunity to assess the ultimatum before a final answer is given. If there's any chance at all of getting him to change the time, it must be done before he gets on television. He won't do it after that."

"You're right. I think you'd better try to get the President on the phone for me while I go to meet with the Cabinet. If you'll let me know when the call comes through, I'll go to the office across the hall and take it there."

The Prime Minister gathered up the papers on his desk and headed for the Cabinet Room. As he entered the dignified, elegant panelled room lined with portraits of past prime ministers, the buzz of conversation ceased abruptly and everyone in the room stood up. Porter went directly to the high-backed chair at the end of the long highly polished table, said, "Thank you, gentlemen," and sat down.

45

With great shuffling and scuffling of chairs, the ministers seated themselves at the table in order of seniority, with the deputy ministers and other staff ranged round the outside of the room.

The Prime Minister opened the meeting without preliminaries. "Gentlemen, I am sure that by this time all of you have been informed that the President of the United States, on behalf of the government of that country, presented to me in a telephone conversation this morning a three-part ultimatum, the answer to which must be given by Parliament no later than six o'clock tomorrow evening.

"At this moment my staff are trying to get through to the President so that I may speak with him and ask that the time be extended. The President is scheduled to address the United States on television at 12:30. Once he informs the American people of the action he has taken, it will be impossible to get him to extend the time, so if we can't get it done now we won't get it at all.

"As soon as I receive word that the President will speak with me, I'll leave the Cabinet Room to talk to him, but I'll come back here as soon as we're finished. I suggest we watch the President's address here so that I can get your immediate reaction. The CBC are setting up a television camera in the Conference Room next to my office, and I will go on live immediately following the President. Unfortunately I will not have time to consult with you about my response, but I hope you have enough confidence in me to back me up in what I say."

Robert Gendron, the Minister for External Affairs, broke in, "Prime Minister, despite the relatively short time you have held office, I know I can assure you that every one of your colleagues here has the utmost faith in you and will stand behind whatever response you see fit to make." There were immediate cries of "Hear, hear!"

As Gendron was speaking, John Thomas had entered the room. He whispered to the Prime Minister, "The President has agreed to speak with you, but it must be very brief because he is attempting to put the finishing touches to what he is going to say on television. If you come with me now, everything is set up."

The President made his way from the cockpit of the 747 to the circular stairs which took him down to the office in the forward cabin of the aircraft.

When it was built, Air Force One had been designed to make it possible for the President to carry on the nation's business almost as easily from the aircraft as from the White House. At the front, normally the first-class area, the President had his private office. In the midsection was a complex of offices housing the secretarial staff and communications centres for telex and telephone links to the ground, as well as a sophisticated system of computers, radar, ground and satellite communication which linked Air Force One with the military surveillance and communication network. Here, too, was the small, sound-insulated TV studio from which the President would broadcast to the nation. At the rear of the aircraft were the President's sleeping quarters and accommodation for the staff.

As he came down the stairs, the President could see Irving Wolf and Al Johnston sitting opposite each other at a desk on the port side of the aircraft. These were his two top advisers. Through them the President maintained his contact with the world. From them came the ideas, analyses, considerations and judgments upon which the man in the world's top position of power had to rely.

Wolf got up and moved towards him, breaking off an

animated discussion with Johnston. He was clutching a sheaf of papers. "We've been having an argument on one or two points, Mr. President."

The President smiled. "I can certainly see that, Irving."

Wolf looked slightly embarrassed. "I guess you can, but this is an important statement we're putting together, and we just aren't seeing eye to eye on it."

The President reached for the papers in Wolf's hand and said, "If you two didn't have different opinions, neither one of you would be worth a damn to me. Let's see what it's all about."

Suddenly there was a startled shout from Al Johnston. "For God's sake, look at that! What the hell do they think they're doing?" He was looking out the window on the port side, just a little ahead of where the President and Wolf were standing by the staircase. The President went immediately to the window.

A fighter aircraft was there, its wing-tip fitted closely under the wing of the 747. He recognized the plane immediately. It was a Canadian CF5 fighter, one of the American-designed, Canadian-built aircraft that had come down the production line in the early 70's. The fighter pilot, whoever he was, certainly knew how to fly. The CF5 was tucked in solid as a rock, just as if it was tied to the 747. The plane gleamed silver in the sunlight, its maple leaf markings boldly defined, and a blazing white vapour trail stretched out behind it. To the President it was a spectacular sight.

Suddenly a thought struck him. He went quickly over to the starboard side of the aircraft and looked out toward the wing-tip. Johnston followed. Sure enough, there was another CF5 in exactly the same position. The President was almost beside himself with admiration and envy. Without taking his eyes off the CF5 he said, "Al, that's one

49

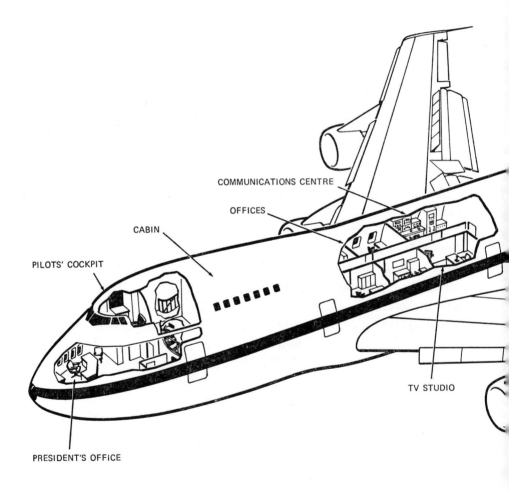

COMMUNICATIONS CENTRE

OFFICES

CABIN

PILOTS' COCKPIT

TV STUDIO

PRESIDENT'S OFFICE

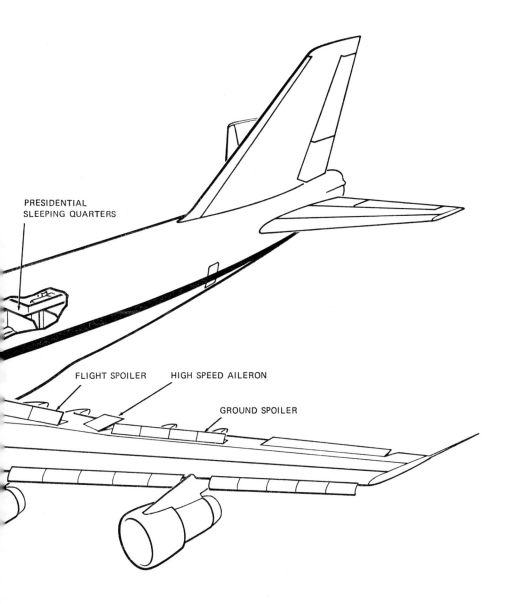

PRESIDENTIAL
SLEEPING QUARTERS

FLIGHT SPOILER   HIGH SPEED AILERON

GROUND SPOILER

of the most beautiful sights in the world. Look at the way that boy's flying that airplane!"

Johnston, who was not an airman, could only say, "How the hell can we get those bastards away from us? They're going to kill us for sure."

The President patted his right shoulder reassuringly. "Don't you fuss, Al. The boy in that plane knows exactly what he's doing. I'm going to try to talk to him." He walked forward to a telephone sitting on the desk and punched the button marked "Captain." When Wypich responded he said, "Mike, I want to talk to those two boys sitting on your wing-tips."

"What two boys?"

"Haven't you seen them? We've got two of the neatest, shiniest CF5's you've ever seen, one on each wing-tip. I guess they're a bit far back for you to spot."

There was a pause. "Well, I'll be damned. I guess those are the two aircraft that Boston Control reported to us about three minutes ago, just as you were leaving the flight deck, Mr. President."

"Must be, Mike. It looks as if the Canadians are telling us we're over their real estate. Try to make contact, will you?"

"Yes, sir. Stand by one."

The President could hear the captain talking to his co-pilot. "What's the serial number of the aircraft on the starboard side?"

"It's 411."

Then the captain transmitted, "Canforce 411, this is Air Force One on 117.8. Do you read me?"

Immediately a voice came back. "Air Force One, this is Canforce 411. Good morning. We're instructed to welcome you and your distinguished passenger to Canada. My wing man and I will fly with you for the next half hour, then you'll be picked up by two other aircraft from my base. We will have someone with you all the way to Resolute, purely as a matter of courtesy, you understand, Colonel Wypich."

The President, listening to the conversation, grinned broadly when the fighter pilot casually let it be known that he knew the name of the captain of the 747. He spoke into his telephone, "Mike, can I transmit using this telephone?"

"Yes, Mr. President. Just push the button on the top right-hand corner."

The President pushed the button, and looking out the window at the sleek fighter said, "Canforce 411, good morning. This is the President speaking. Give me your ident, please."

"Good morning, sir. I'm Colonel Jack Prince. I command the Canadian forces base at Bagotville, Quebec. I was instructed by Ottawa to take charge of this escort operation. On the port wing-tip is Lieutenant Colonel Jean Belisle. He commands 433 squadron at Bagotville."

Belisle broke in. "Good morning, sir."

"Good morning, son. We're sure glad to have you boys along. We're going from here across to Churchill. First I want to take a look at the big new deep-water port you people are building up there. Then I'm going straight north to Resolute."

Colonel Prince's voice came back. "Sorry we won't be going all the way, sir. We'll be with you for the next half hour, then you'll be picked up by another team."

"Fine, Colonel, fine," responded the President. "But now I'd be obliged if you'd do me a favour. My staff on this big bird aren't really used to seeing airplanes fly so close and they're getting a little uptight about it. It doesn't bother me one bit, but I'd appreciate it if you'd park your aircraft about two hundred yards out in battle formation. It would make everybody here just a little more comfortable."

"Wilco, sir," said the Colonel, and passed the word to his wing man. "Battle formation, Jean. Go!"

With that, both fighters turned outward. The Colonel took up his position about two hundred yards abreast of Air Force One on the starboard side, while Belisle's aircraft did the same on the port.

As the President put down the telephone Wypich entered the cabin from the cockpit. "Sir, you mentioned Churchill to the Canadian pilots but I don't have that in your instructions."

"That's right, Mike. It struck me as I talked to those young fellows that we would be passing pretty close to Churchill, so I thought it would be a good idea just to go by and take a look at the new port from low level. When we get there let's go down to about two thousand feet and then head for Resolute."

The captain said, "Yes, sir," and went back up the circular stairs.

The President walked over and sat down beside his aides. "O.K., Irving," he said. "The pilots have given us lots of room. Now you two can relax."

Wolf nodded. "Here's your speech, Mr. President. Your rough draft was excellent in parts but, if you'll pardon the expression, pretty damn awful in others. When you read this draft you'll probably say I've screwed up the excellent parts and left in the bad ones. Anyway, here it is."

The President smiled. He found Irving's dry wit refreshing.

Wolf had first impressed him more than a decade earlier when he had testified before the Senate Foreign Relations Committee regarding the pressure being brought to bear on the United States by the OPEC countries. On that occasion, Wolf had presented a superb exposé of the increasingly-difficult and complex problem confronted

54

by the U.S. in its relationship with the Organization of Petroleum Exporting Countries. Many of these nations were Arab and, as Wolf had skilfully explained, had combined to exert leverage on the United States to cease supporting Israel by supplying it with money and military equipment.

After the testimony, the Senator had sought out Wolf, befriended him and asked for the opportunity, readily granted by Wolf, to consult with him from time to time on questions of international trade and world diplomacy. So it was only natural that when he began his drive for the presidency he invite Irving Wolf to become part of the team. After the election, the President selected Wolf, not as a member of the Cabinet but as his special assistant and adviser on a broad range of matters assigned to him. With that recognition, real power came into the hands of Irving Wolf, power which he did not hesitate to use.

When the native people of the Northwest Territories and Yukon had begun, only a few days before, to blow up sections of the Mackenzie pipeline, it was Wolf who had recognized that the President would have to take action immediately to protect American interests in the area. It was Wolf who proposed the ultimatum and who drafted its terms. Despite the President's reluctance, Wolf had convinced him and the Cabinet at the meeting which had taken place the evening before, and it was Wolf who had secured agreement on the strategy of sanctions which the President could impose to enforce the ultimatum.

Now he sat watching the President, his scythe-like nose pinched between his index fingers, a gesture of contemplation for which he was now famous. He was not worried that the President would reject or alter the draft speech; that seldom happened. Rather he was considering the implications of the economic sanctions he had proposed

55

against Canada, the first of which was to take effect at twelve noon.

As he expected, the President, when he had finished reading, took off his glasses, sat back and put his hands behind his head. After a few moments' silence he drawled, "That's fine, Irving. Looks good to me. But I tell you I'm still not happy about threatening to put a bullet between the eyes of the Canadians. It makes me very uneasy. I'm concerned about the ultimatum, and I'm concerned about the sanctions."

He stood up. "However, we've done it, and we'll stick by it. How much time have we got until I do the broadcast?"

Wolf looked at his watch and said, "Seventeen minutes, Mr. President. The networks have cleared you for 12:30. The TV studio back there is all set."

"You mean aft, Irving, not back," the President chuckled. "Don't forget, you're on a ship."

Wolf smiled and shrugged. "The studio aft is all set. They've got the Presidental Seal in place and the flag behind the table so that everybody who is watching you will think you're right in the White House. They'll get a hell of a shock when they find out you've been broadcasting from Air Force One over Canadian territory via the Canadian satellite Anik 3."

"Why are we using that satellite and not one of our own?"

"Oh, I gather the orbit is a little better for our position and the transmission will be clearer. Some time ago we rented two of the surplus TV channels on Anik 3. We'll use one of them this morning."

As the President turned toward the tail of the aircraft, Al Johnston came up behind him and said, "Mr. President, Prime Minister Porter wants to speak with you. His office says it's very urgent."

56

The President checked his watch. "There isn't much time. It'll have to be short." He followed Johnston back to the telephone. Johnston picked it up.

"Senator Thomas, the President will speak with the Prime Minister but it's got to be short because, as you know, he's going to address the nation in a very few moments."

Senator Thomas' voice came back. "We understand. I'll get the PM. Hang on, please."

In a few seconds the Prime Minister came on the line. When he was on, the President took the telephone from his aide and the two exchanged terse greetings.

The President said, "What can I do for you?"

Porter replied, "You gave me an arbitrary deadline of six o'clock tomorrow night. I've talked to my people here and I don't know if we can get Parliament reconvened and all the steps properly taken in such a short time so that I can give you an answer which reflects the view of the people of Canada. The Arctic question is not a new one. We've been haggling over it for years, and in the interests of fairness I think you should give us more time, even an additional twenty-four hours."

The President replied quickly, "I expected you'd be back to me on this point, and I've already discussed it thoroughly with my advisers. The answer has got to be No, there can be no extension. I've given you an ultimatum, and I've given you what I consider to be a reasonable length of time for your decision-making process to function. There's no way that, having stipulated at nine o'clock in the morning what the United States wants, I'm going to start backing off three hours later. No, Mr. Prime Minister, the terms of the ultimatum stand and the timing with it. Furthermore, just to show you that we mean business, at twelve noon the Secretary of the Treasury was instructed to place an immediate embargo on the movement of any and all U.S. investment or other funds into Canada. At the present rate, that will mean a cut-off of $30-million of capital investment money a day. That's just for openers."

The Prime Minister started to protest but the President cut him short, "I'm sorry, Mr. Prime Minister, I'm due on television in just a few minutes, as you know. My staff tell me that you are going to respond as soon as I have finished. All I can say is, Be careful!"

He hung up.

As the President and Wolf entered the communications cabin the five men manning it glanced up, then carried on with their work. Pete Young, the President's Television Director, was giving final instructions at the main control console, so the President and Wolf waited, looking around at the familiar but still amazing setup.

Against the port wall were banks of telex equipment carrying reports from the State Department, the Pentagon, and the news wires. Two of the crew monitored these messages at all times, and delivered batches of the most significant items to the President's secretarial staff at half-hour intervals. Ranged against the forward wall were the high-frequency radio transmitters and receivers. To the President's left, under the arched roof of the cabin, were the computer terminal and control units which were hooked into the master defence computer system at the Pentagon. Through this terminal the President alone could issue the final command codes for missile interception or even nuclear retaliation. To the rear of the cabin, behind a glass panel, the President could see the TV studio, with its three cameras set up facing the desk, complete with Presidential Seal and Flag.

When Peter Young had completed his work at the control console he looked up and nodded.

58

"All ready to go, Pete?" the President asked.

"All set, Mr. President. We're locked on to the satellite, we've run a transmission check, everything looks good. The networks are standing by. There'll also be a feed-in to all the Canadian networks."

"That's good, Pete. How much time have we got?"

"Two minutes and thirty seconds, Mr. President."

"I guess I'd better get in there." The President headed for the studio door. In a few moments he was installed behind the desk with his papers in front of him.

Young flicked a switch on the console. "Are you all set, Mr. President?"

"Yes, Pete."

"Would you give me your voice level please, sir?"

"O.K. I'll do it by asking you to give me the countdown as we come up to 12:30. I understand that, as usual, you'll show the Presidential Seal for five seconds and do the intro over the Seal."

"Right. We're coming up to fifteen seconds. All network clearances established. Coming up to ten seconds . . . five, four, three, two, one." He flicked the switch for transmission of the Presidential Seal and spoke into the microphone in front of him. "Ladies and gentlemen, the President of the United States." Then he switched to the President and pointed to him.

"My fellow Americans, I want to inform all of you about certain actions I have decided to take to meet the serious energy crisis which confronts this nation. . . ."

Ottawa / 12:25 p.m., EDT

Following his phone call to the President, Robert Porter stood for a moment deep in thought, his head down, shoulders slumped. Then he turned and walked slowly back into the Cabinet Room. The din of many voices ceased abruptly as he entered. The tension and anger shown on his face told his colleagues what had happened even before he began to speak.

"The President has given a flat No to my request for an extension of time. Furthermore, the United States has gone further than I thought they would at this stage to show us that they mean business. He has, as of twelve noon today, instructed the Secretary of the Treasury to place an immediate embargo on the movement of all U.S. investment capital into Canada."

The voice of young Michael Clarkson, the Minister of Finance, broke through the shouts of outrage which greeted this announcement. "The country can't survive without that capital!"

The Prime Minister hesitated a moment, then replied, "Now listen to me. We can survive, and we must, Michael. We've got to show at once that we will not be intimidated. Since the President has chosen to invoke sanctions against us even before the expiry of his deadline, he'd better learn that sanctions can go both ways. You should instruct your deputy, Angus Stone, and the Governor of the Bank of Canada — are they both here? — ah, yes, gentlemen —

you should instruct them right now to take all necessary steps to prevent the transfer of any Canadian funds into the United States, directly or indirectly. I have in mind dividends, return of capital, investment money, and the like. And all the stock exchanges should be directed to cease trading immediately and to remain closed until further notice."

The two financial officials huddled briefly with the Minister, then quickly left the room.

Glancing at his watch, the Prime Minister pressed a button under the table in front of him to activate the large television set mounted high on the wall at the far end of the room. As the panelling slid quietly open, the screen was already showing the words, "Special Bulletin, Stand By." Porter said, "Now gentlemen, our time is short. During the President's address, if a point occurs to you which you think I should cover in my response, make a note and pass it up to me. I want to have the benefit of your ideas and I'll try to incorporate any point you wish me to make.

"As soon as I have finished my televised statement, I'll come back here so that we can discuss the entire situation and make some decisions as to how the matter should be handled. As you know, I have taken steps to recall Parliament, bring in the provincial premiers, and hold a briefing session at eight o'clock tomorrow morning, to be followed by an emergency sitting of the House at twelve noon."

At this point the Presidential Seal flashed on the screen. Porter pressed the button to bring up the volume.

"Ladies and gentlemen, the President of the United States."

The President's familiar craggy countenance appeared on the screen. He displayed no sign of nervousness; he was, as always, calm and confident, a man who wore power with

61

dignity, directness, and assurance. Years before, when he had been first a senator and then a member of the Cabinet, he had had no hesitation in voicing tough and sharply critical views of Canada. He clearly considered Canada a bothersome colonial attachment to the United States' empire, worth putting up with only because of its rich treasury of mineral and fossil fuel resources. Everyone in the room knew he was watching a man who would pay no attention to Canada or the Canadian point of view, when they came into conflict with U.S. interests.

The President began, "My fellow Americans: I want to inform all of you about certain actions I have decided to take to meet the serious energy crisis which confronts this nation.

"This morning at nine o'clock Washington time, I telephoned the Prime Minister of Canada to discuss with him the urgency of the situation. I pointed out that this winter approximately 20% of all the industries in the United States which rely upon natural gas would have to be shut down. I made it plain to him that hospitals would have to be closed, that homes and apartments would be without heat, and that the American people would suffer, and indeed many would die this winter, because of a shortage of natural gas in the United States.

"My fellow Americans, the responsibility for this shortage rests primarily on the shoulders of the Canadians.

"The Canadians have vast reserves of natural gas in their Arctic regions, especially in the Mackenzie Delta and on the Arctic Islands. Because Canada could not put up the necessary capital, United States' money has paid for the construction of a pipeline to bring gas from Mackenzie and Prudhoe Bay in Alaska down to the Chicago and Detroit areas, one of the most critically affected regions of this country.

"Since 1970, American firms have poured millions upon millions of dollars into exploration and development. To date, more than 60-trillion cubic feet in proven reserves of natural gas has been discovered in the Arctic Islands alone.

"Because the Mackenzie pipeline will not meet all our requirements, Tenneco and the other major United States gas distribution firms, which have financed the discoveries in the Islands, are prepared to buy gas at the well-head and to create their own transportation system to deliver it to United States markets.

"For the past three years, American scientists have been carrying out an extremely costly and dangerous experiment to test a prototype pipeline system to transport gas between the Arctic Islands under water. As an alternative solution, we have spent approximately one billion dollars to develop a prototype Resources Carrier aircraft which has just been test-flown at the Boeing factory in Seattle. When fully operational, this aircraft, three times the size of a Boeing 747, will be capable of carrying 2¼-million pounds of liquid natural gas. Although the Canadians at one time had contracts which would have allowed them to control the building, financing and operation of these aircraft, they were once again unable to muster the initiative and financial resources to carry through with the project, and we have therefore taken it over. To sum up, American know-how, and American dollars, have discovered nearly all the reserves of natural gas. We need that gas desperately, right now. American engineering has developed the facilities to bring it to market. This is a great achievement, and we have every right to be proud of what we have accomplished.

"Why, then, do we find ourselves facing the present energy crisis? Quite simply, the Canadian government refuses to let us have any of the natural gas on the Arctic Islands. Negotiating teams from the United States government have been attempting for years to work out an agreement with the Canadians to purchase one-third of the crude reserves on the Islands, that is to say, 20-trillion cubic feet. At the same time, we have been trying to establish a comprehensive continental energy policy under which both countries would have mutual access to all of the electricity, crude oil, natural gas, nuclear power, and any other sources of energy which might be available.

"Unfortunately, we have been totally unsuccessful in our dealings with the Canadians, not because they have at any time said No to our legitimate requests, but because the Canadian bureaucracy is in such a state of division that they find it impossible to agree on a course of action which they are prepared to present to their political masters.

"The result is that no Canadian government since 1970, when the first evidence of the growing energy crisis began to emerge, has been able to come to grips with the reasonable demands of the United States for a commitment on the gas of the Arctic Islands or a continental energy agreement. Despite our eagerness to work out a plan which would be to the benefit of all Canadians, Americans and American industry are now facing an intolerable situation because of the inability of departments of the Canadian government to work with each other.

"Canada is a country which has long been regarded as a friendly trading and cultural partner of the United States. Most of its major manufacturing industries are subsidiaries of multi-national U.S.-controlled firms, and most of its resource industries, including minerals such as nickel and iron, which are essential to the United States, are controlled by American interests. Furthermore, much of the high standard of living enjoyed by the Canadian people must be directly credited to their favoured position as the first and largest trading partner of the United States.

"Under all these circumstances, it is not unreasonable for you and me as American citizens to expect, when we are suffering from a shortage of a commodity which the Canadians have in abundance, that they should adopt an open-handed policy.

"I have referred earlier to the Mackenzie Valley pipeline. I must now tell you that approximately ten days ago I was informed that acts of sabotage were occurring along the pipeline route. Let me give you the background.

"When large-scale oil development began in Alaska, almost a decade ago, the United States government recognized the legitimate demands of the native people to a share in the natural wealth of their land. We made a settlement with the native people of $500-million in cash, and 40-million acres of land. And we provided an additional $500-million to come from a 2% royalty on all the gas and oil production from Prudhoe Bay. This was a fair and a just settlement.

"Unfortunately, despite our strong recommendations, the Canadian government has refused to settle justly and fairly with their native peoples. Even now, as the Mackenzie Valley line nears completion, no settlement of any kind has taken place. As a result, the radicals within the native peoples' organizations have begun to blow up the pipeline.

"There is little the Canadian government can do to prevent these acts of sabotage, and it is clear that in American interests as well as Canadian a settlement must be reached at once.

"And so, my fellow Americans, time has run out in our

negotiations with Canada. The United States can no longer tolerate either a failure or a refusal by Canada to come to terms concerning natural gas and to settle their problems with their own people so that gas can be delivered to meet American needs. I am sure none of you would wish me to be harsh or vindictive with the Canadian government. On the other hand, it is my responsibility as your President to press the United States' case in the most direct and forthright manner.

"In the face of this emergency, I have been forced to take strong action. After receiving advice from the leaders of the Senate and the House of Representatives, and after conferring with the Chief Justice of the United States, I took the following steps at nine o'clock this morning. . . ."

As the President described the ultimatum he had given to the Prime Minister, Porter was rapidly making notes. His colleagues sat watching the President transfixed. Some scribbled short notes which were passed up to the Prime Minister. No one spoke.

Now there was no way back. The President had informed his people and the world that the U.S. demands would have to be met.

The President was moving to the conclusion of his address. "I have stipulated that unconditional, affirmative answers must be given to each of these three requirements no later than six o'clock tomorrow evening. We have prepared a series of economic sanctions which can be invoked against Canada should our reasonable ultimatum be refused. My fellow Americans, it is in your interests and in the interests of stopping this needless suffering by our people that I am fully prepared to impose such sanctions should it be necessary.

"In order to demonstrate our firm resolve in this matter, I have instructed the appropriate government officials that as of twelve noon today an embargo should be placed on the transfer of any funds by United States persons or corporations into Canada. This includes the lending of money, the purchase of shares or securities, or any other method of investment. Canada needs these monies from the United States in order to survive economically. By the same token, the United States needs access to the Arctic Islands natural gas in order to survive economically and physically. The principle is the same in both cases — survival.

"In conclusion I wish to say to the Canadian people that the United States wishes none of you individually any harm whatsoever. If there is any difference between us, it is not between our peoples but rather between our respective governments. Americans deeply regret that you must now be called upon to suffer for the ineptitude and stubbornness of an inflexible and unimaginative bureaucracy which has your new federal government paralyzed by its incompetence.

"And to the world I say that the United States and Canada must resolve this crisis between us. Interference or involvement by other nations is unnecessary and unacceptable.

"My fellow Americans, this great nation, the finest country in the world and the largest and most powerful, was founded and lives upon the fundamental principles of liberty and justice for all. I am sure that you will want me to maintain those principles in our dealings with Canada over the next few hours, but I want each of you to understand that I have first in mind the health and well-being of every American citizen. The interests of the United States and its citizens must be upheld.

"Thank you, and good afternoon."

Someone on the Prime Minister's right muttered, "Bullshit!"

For a few moments after the first outburst, there was silence in the Cabinet chamber. Then bedlam broke loose. Everyone was talking at once.

The Prime Minister sat, oblivious to the noise around him, rapidly making notes. Abruptly he got up and left the room, followed by Senator Thomas. Cries of "Give him hell, Bob" and "Don't submit to blackmail" followed him as he went out the door.

As he reached the Conference room, he was met by Tom Scott, who reported that everything was set. The conference table had been moved toward one end of the room opposite the TV camera and a chair placed behind it so the Prime Minister would be facing the camera with a panelled wall as background.

The producer, Al Price, who had covered many of the Prime Minister's speeches, was well known to Porter. They exchanged greetings.

Price said, "Would you sit over here, sir? We've got the camera set up to cover you face on. You can put your notes on the table in front of you." He led the Prime Minister around behind the long conference table and slipped a neck microphone over his head. Porter sat down and glanced at his notes.

"How much time do we have?"

"You're on in thirty seconds, sir."

The cameraman and the other two crewmen, who had

been muttering among themselves, quieted down. The Prime Minister took off his glasses, and with an automatic motion put them in his left shirt pocket. He sat up a little straighter and looked the camera in the eye. He was ready.

Al Price held up his outspread hand. "Five seconds." At the final cue, he pointed to the Prime Minister.

"The President of the United States has just informed the American people — and those in Canada who were able to see or hear him — of the ultimatum which he presented to me and the government of Canada this morning.

"Originally I had planned to speak with you this evening at nine o'clock. I still intend to do so, because by that time the situation will be much clearer and the steps taken by your government to meet this crisis will be firmly established. However, when I learned that the President was going to address the American nation at this time, I felt it appropriate to follow his statement with one of my own.

"As the President pointed out, the people of the United States are indeed caught in a severe energy crisis. Some years ago it became apparent that because of bad planning, or failure to provide for future energy needs, heavy shortages of oil, natural gas and electricity were about to occur. The first serious shortage was felt in the winter of 1972, when some factories, schools, and other institutions in various parts of the United States were shut down because of lack of fuel. You are all aware, I am sure, of the continuing problems which have increased since that time, of electrical "brown-outs," of gasoline rationing and of shortages of heating fuels, which have occurred regularly, winter and summer, since that time. During this period two things have happened: First, the population of the United States has grown rapidly over the last decade from 209-million to about 229-million this year, an increase almost equivalent to Canada's entire present population. In other words, the energy needs of the United States at this time is at least equal to its 1970 needs plus the entire energy requirements of Canada.

"During this time, the United States has continued to expand its industrial and manufacturing capacity without restraint, thereby further increasing its insatiable demand for energy.

"The United States moved as quickly as it could to overcome the energy crisis. It was successful in increasing its supply of crude oil but not in obtaining additional natural gas. That is the reason why the United States is much more concerned about getting its hands on Canada's natural gas resources than on the crude oil reserves that have also been found in the Mackenzie Delta and in our Arctic Islands.

"The Americans have been able to keep up with their oil demands as they have risen because they have been able to purchase crude oil from various places in the world such as Venezuela, Algeria and the Middle East, and to transport it in the fleet of oil tankers which they began to build in the 60's.

"The situation regarding natural gas is more complicated. The background is simply this: Natural gas represents a little over 30 per cent of the energy consumed by the United States on an annual basis. At the beginning of this decade, there was a shortage of natural gas amounting to 900-billion cubic feet per year. Today the figure is more than two and a half times that amount.

"The world appears to have adequate reserves of natural gas available, and the problem facing the Americans is not that there is a short supply but that there is no adequate transportation system in existence which can carry the natural gas to the United States from overseas.

"Tankers of the kind necessary to transport natural gas are still in very short supply. The gas must be cooled to the point at which it becomes liquid (−260°F), and it must be kept at that intense cold in special uncontaminated containers during transportation. The tankers required to carry liquid natural gas did not even exist a decade ago, and though the Americans and Japanese are building them as quickly as they can, there are still very few in operation. The Americans have twenty, but they could use a hundred.

"In the light of this situation, the United States has no choice but to make every effort to gain immediate access to the reserves in the Mackenzie Delta and the Arctic Islands, where it is possible to transport the gas by pipeline or the special airlift tankers to which the President referred.

"Let me say to all Canadians and to every American that I have great sympathy for the dilemma in which the President finds himself and for the American people.

"When I came to the office of Prime Minister only seven weeks ago, I took on the legacy of action or inaction of all my predecessors of whatever party. I fault none of them. On the other hand, there is little doubt that the President is quite correct when he complains of the inaction of the Canadian bureaucracy. That bureaucracy is the product of a system which has given the country great stability and has permitted the various government departments to function effectively despite frequent political shifts. But inevitably over the years the system has become excessively rigid. It has failed to keep pace with the changing times. I've proposed to make a number of reforms in this area, but that is a matter for discussion on another occasion.

"The point is this. Canada must accept some of the blame for the failure of which we stand accused by the President. We *have* been negligent in dealing with our native people. It is perfectly clear that they have a moral

71

right to share in the returns from the resources of their lands, and we should have dealt with them long ago. And we did, in fact, fail to make an arrangement with the Americans to give them access to the Canadian Arctic Islands gas. In part, this was due to a natural concern that our own requirements should be taken into consideration, but in part it was also a failure to come to grips with what was obviously an emergency situation. The President is right. Canada is largely to blame.

"But having conceded this, the question remains: Is the President justified in suddenly giving Canada an ultimatum and enforcing that ultimatum by economic reprisals even before the deadline? This question is of major concern to me. I do not propose to attempt to answer it at this time, but I will do so when the House of Commons meets in emergency session tomorrow."

The Prime Minister then outlined the steps which had already been taken to recall Parliament, to consult with the provincial premiers, and to brief the members of the Senate and the House of Commons prior to the emergency sitting of the House the following afternoon. Then he continued.

"There is no doubt that this is the most difficult and important crisis Canada has ever faced. What the outcome will be I cannot predict, but I am most anxious that the Canadian people remain calm, that there should be no panic, and that there should be no reaction of an anti-American nature. Any acts of physical retaliation against any United States citizen in Canada would cause irreparable damage to our already-delicate position in relation to the United States.

"I ask every journalist, editor and copy writer to maintain a high calibre of responsible, factual reporting of the news and to refrain from any kind of comment which might inflame emotions.

"This is a time when the nation and its leaders should abandon partisan positions or regional attitudes, so that we can all reply to the United States with one voice.

"This crisis demands of all of us courage, strength, and patriotism. I am sure the Canadian people will respond."

The Prime Minister then spoke in French, covering the same ground. Finally he said, "I have asked the radio and television networks to permit me to speak with you again tonight at nine o'clock. At that time I will review the situation as it then exists.

"Thank you."

The two ravens flew soundlessly overhead in the brilliant sunlight of the early afternoon as Sam and Bessie trekked along the pipeline cutting. The two enormous black birds had joined them early on the first day, and Sam had recognized their presence as a good omen. They were his favourite birds, and among the most intelligent. They live and fly usually in pairs, talking to each other much like crows but in a more guttural fashion. They make a good team. In the settlements of the treed parts of the Arctic they are the scavengers which scour the communities and keep them much cleaner than they would otherwise be.

They particularly delight in driving the husky dogs mad. A pair of ravens can strip a dog of his food in the twinkling of an eye, one landing in front of the dog just beyond the length of his chain, flapping his wings and muttering obscenities at the animal. With great howling, barking, and mighty pulls against the restraining chain, the dog uses all his efforts to get at the bird to destroy it, forgetting all about his food. The more frantic he becomes, the louder the raven shouts at him, and goads him on.

Meanwhile, just behind the frustrated dog, the second raven is quietly but quickly gulping down his dinner, pausing once in a while only long enough to smile quickly up at the wild, well-plotted scene. When it is finished, the two birds fly swiftly off, leaving the dog hungry, frustrated and angry.

"Yes," Sam thought, "two ravens make a pretty good team, and if Bessie and I can get these last two bombs set up, we'll have done a good job too. At least we'll wake up those northerners in Ottawa who keep forgetting there are people up here."

Ottawa / 1:03 p.m., EDT

As the Prime Minister and Senator Thomas returned to the Cabinet Room, there was a wave of applause and congratulation as everyone stood while the Prime Minister moved to his chair at the head of the table. When the commotion had died down, he motioned them to be seated and sat down himself.

"Thank you, gentlemen, I appreciate your support."

"Prime Minister," said the Minister for External Affairs, "you can see that we're pleased with what you said. We support totally the position you took. We're proud that you're the leader of our party at this critical time."

"Thanks, Robert. Thank you all. Now let's get down to business. There's a lot to be done.

"I've told you that there will be a major briefing starting at eight o'clock tomorrow morning. I have asked each of the ministers responsible for the departments most directly concerned to prepare a status paper for presentation at that time. The Ministers for External Affairs, Energy Mines and Resources, Northern Development, Transport, Environment, Finance, and National Defence will all make presentations.

"A question period will follow each briefing. Since we have only three hours, I've suggested that the combined statement and question period should not exceed twenty-five minutes per ministry. I have asked the Minister for External Affairs and his deputy to lead off.

"I met with all the ministers concerned and their deputies this morning. I assume that preparations are now well under way. Is this so, gentlemen?"

The seven ministers and their deputies all nodded.

"Good. The House will sit at twelve noon. I will introduce a motion made jointly by myself, the Leader of the Opposition, and the NDP and Social Credit leaders. I'd like the Minister of Justice to draft the motion.

"Could you do that for us, Ken, in the next few hours?"

Kenneth Locke, down the table on the Prime Minister's right-hand side, said, "Certainly, sir."

The Prime Minister continued. "I suggest, Ken, that the motion restate the ultimatum and move that it be rejected. This of course is a matter of form. The fact that I present it does not necessarily mean I support it. I want to listen to the debate in the House, to hear the briefing, and to talk with quite a number of people before I decide whether to vote for or against the motion. The stakes are far too high for me to make up my mind conclusively one way or the other until I have had a full opportunity to assess every aspect of the situation.

"As soon as you have the motion drafted, Ken, I would be obliged if you would bring it to me. We can work it over together and then perhaps you could take it to the leaders of the other parties for approval or amendment."

Otto Gunther, Minister of Energy, Mines and Resources, spoke up. "Prime Minister, I think it would be appropriate to suggest that the Cabinet have a look at the wording of the motion before it is taken to the leaders of the other parties. While I am quite sure that what you and the Minister of Justice put together will be satisfactory, I think it would give the motion added weight if it carried the approval of the entire Cabinet."

The Prime Minister thought for a moment and then

said, "All right, Otto. Once Ken and I have settled the draft and before it goes to the other parties, copies will be delivered to each of you with instructions that your comments will have to be back in Ken's hands within an hour.

"The final thing that we have to discuss at this point is the list of speakers from our party during the debate on the motion. The number of speakers in each party will be in proportion to the number of seats held in the House. There will be eleven from our party. According to the plan agreed on with the other parties each speaker, apart from the party leaders, will have ten minutes.

"I suggest that James Campbell, as House Leader, be responsible for organizing the speakers for our party.

"Jim, you might want to consider asking all the members who wish to speak to let you know by a certain time. After that, the choice can be made by lot. This may be an unusual approach, but it will be a fair one under the circumstances.

"Now, gentlemen, I've been doing a lot of talking and you've been doing a lot of listening. Do you have any comments on the course of action I've outlined?"

As he was asking this question, Tom Scott entered the room and handed the Prime Minister a note. Porter scanned it briefly and nodded to Scott, who left the room.

Silence had greeted the Prime Minister's invitation to comment.

Gendron of External Affairs broke in. "Obviously, Prime Minister, the fact that there are no questions indicates general agreement with the steps you have proposed. Might I suggest that if any of us do have comments or questions we get in touch with Tom Scott. He can pass anything straight on to you if required."

"Thank you, Bob. That's a good suggestion."

"Well, there's one thing that bothers me, Prime Min-

78

ister." It was Otto Gunther from Newfoundland again, Robert Porter's main competitor at the leadership convention eight weeks before. Gunther's defeat by Porter still rankled. After all, he was an older, more experienced and senior member of the party, and as far as he was concerned Porter was only a johnny-come-lately. "What I don't understand is that you haven't given us any indication of what you think about this ultimatum. It's all very well to say that you want to wait until you've heard the briefing and the debate, but I don't think that's good enough. We're in a difficult situation and you ought to exercise some leadership and give the country some direction."

Porter smiled a tight, hard smile. "I suppose what you're saying, Otto, is that if you were the Prime Minister you'd be telling us where to go."

"You're damn right I would. The leader of this country has to be prepared to show where he stands, not wait for somebody else to make up his mind in a debate." Otto Gunther returned the smile, but he meant what he said.

Porter nodded. "I understand your point of view, but I must say I don't agree with it. I feel very strongly that I should stand by my intention of hearing and considering every opinion and every factor before I state my position.

"Now, gentlemen, if there are no other comments, I have one final thing. In my television talk I spoke about the importance of keeping calm and unemotional. May I suggest that when you are talking with the press you make no derogatory remarks about the United States, the President, or the action they are taking. Anything you or I say at this time which is inflammatory can only serve to harm the interests of Canada, and severely damage our ability to negotiate.

"I have just received word that the Governor-General has arrived from Victoria. I want to see him as soon as

79

possible, so I will leave the meeting in the hands of the Minister for External Affairs. Thank you."

Neither Robert Porter nor John Thomas spoke as they walked quickly back to the Prime Minister's office. There Porter called his secretary and instructed her to have his car ready and standing by in front of the East Block. Then he asked Tom Scott to phone Government House and find out whether His Excellency could receive him in about twenty minutes.

Scott replied, "I'll do that right away, sir, but first I should tell you that the Chief of the Defence Staff called about two minutes ago and said that he had information he wanted to pass on to you personally."

"O.K., have somebody get him on the line for me as soon as possible."

As he turned away from the intercom, Thomas said, "I don't know about you, Bob, but I'm hungry as hell. Do you think we could have something sent in? We haven't had a thing to eat, not even coffee."

Porter laughed. "Too bad, John, you probably could stand to lose a few pounds anyhow. I don't think I'm going to have anything, but I'll get my secretary to find some sandwiches and coffee for you.

"While I'm seeing the Governor-General, do you think you could rough out a sketch of what I might say in my television address tonight? I want to tell the people exactly what's going on and how we propose to deal with the situation, and I want to stress again the need for a calm approach. You might get Bob Gendron of External Affairs to give you a hand. He's a pretty wise old bird, and he's had lots of experience. Also, he understands the Americans very well."

"Sure, at least I'll make a stab at it. I can't guarantee anything, but having listened to you for a good part of the

80

day and watched what's going on, I'm sure I can get something down on paper. It won't be the first speech I've drafted for you."

"Thanks, I'd appreciate it."

Porter turned to gaze out the office window. "I've got something else on my mind. I wonder how we could get a good reading of what the people of Canada think we should do about this ultimatum. Surely with the fantastic communications systems today there must be some way to do a representative sampling of opinion fast. Maybe Davies of Bell Telephone would have an idea. He's a good friend of mine. You know him, don't you?"

"Yes, I do. I met him in Montreal with you just before the leadership campaign started. We had lunch at the Beaver Club in the Queen Elizabeth."

The intercom buzzed. It was Tom Scott. "Sir, the Chief of the Defence Staff, General Adamson, is on the line."

"Thanks, Tom."

The Prime Minister picked up the telephone. "General, you were calling me."

The General answered. "Yes, sir. Two things: First of all, I want to report that the airlift for the members of Parliament and the Senate is going very well. We should have everyone in for the eight o'clock briefing tomorrow morning except for those who are too ill to travel — there are a couple — and three from the Senate who are out of the country and can't make it back in time."

"That's a very good turnout."

"The second thing is that I think you should know that in the past twenty-four hours we have noticed a substantial increase in the number of practice flights carried out by USAF bombers over Canadian territory. The same thing applies to fighter interception practice. As you know, Prime Minister, under the NORAD arrangements, the Americans have to get final clearance from us to over-fly Canadian territory. They've been doing this, so there's no secret about the flights, but I thought I ought to draw the matter to your attention.

"We have no intelligence that there is any ground activity, troop movements, or anything of that kind anywhere in the United States, but there certainly is a lot of activity in the air."

"Thank you for telling me, General. The President knew very well that you would report to me the increase in the overflights. Obviously it's another piece of pressure.

"Since I have you on the line, General, there's a matter I should take up with you. I have been quite concerned that the military be ready to come to the aid of the civil power should any anti-American reaction develop in the next few hours — protest parades, or acts of violence against American citizens or property in Canada. I understand that the emergency structure that was set up in the early 70's after the FLQ trouble in Quebec is designed to cope with this kind of situation, and I just want to make sure that the military are on the alert."

The CDS responded, "We certainly are, sir. I've already issued instructions and the machinery is in operation. I've kept the Minister of Defence and his deputy fully informed, including the information I have just passed on to you, sir. They have approved of what we're doing."

"Thank you, General. Keep a close eye on the situation. For what it is worth, I think the Canadian mouse should put all its military forces on the alert in case the American elephant decides to get nasty, although I can't conceive of such a possibility."

The General chuckled. "I will, sir."

The Prime Minister hung up and said to Thomas, "I guess you could gather what that was all about. The Americans are rattling their planes at us. And the members and senators are on their way back.

"Now I should be off."

He touched the intercom. "Tom, is my car ready?"

"Yes, sir, and there are four RCMP officers here waiting to escort you through the gang of reporters and photographers lying in wait out in the hall."

"O.K., I'm leaving right now."

As he headed for the door, Porter said to Thomas, "I suggest you stay and work here, John, rather than go back to your own office. You can use any of my staff. But suit yourself."

The Prime Minister went through the reception area, where he collected the four RCMP officers, resplendent in their traditional red-coated uniforms. Two of the men preceded him and the other two walked one on each side.

As they opened the door to the corridor, the Prime Minister was confronted by a mass of pushing reporters, most of them holding out microphones. All were shouting questions, none of which he could make out. The Prime Minister and his bodyguard wedged their way through the milling throng to the top of the staircase, but there they were blocked. Finally Porter held his hands in the air and waved vigorously. Gradually the commotion died down and the shoving subsided. The RCMP officers cleared a space of a few feet between the Prime Minister and the reporters, but he still had to shout to be heard.

"If you will all be quiet for a minute, I'll tell you what I am doing and where I am going. There's no time for interviews at this point."

A score of hungry microphones were thrust toward the Prime Minister, and television cameras ground away.

"The Governor-General has just arrived back from Victoria and I am on my way to advise him of the ultimatum and to let him know what steps the government is taking. Also, of course, I will seek his advice. I've known His Excellency for many years and there is no man in the country whose counsel I would value more at a time such as this.

"I have nothing more to add to what I said on television a short while ago except that all the machinery is in operation to ensure that a decision will be made by Parliament within the time frame set down by the United States."

Someone shouted, "How are you going to vote on the ultimatum question, Prime Minister?"

Porter did not respond immediately. When he did, he spoke slowly. "I am not in a position to say how I will vote, and will not be until the House has completed its debate tomorrow afternoon. By that time I will have heard what the members of the House have to say, I will have had opinions from all across the country, and I will have had counsel from the premiers of the provinces. When I finish off the debate in the House tomorrow, you will know my decision on the ultimatum."

Another question. "Prime Minister, do you think the Americans are justified in putting a gun to our heads?"

This was a question that the Prime Minister clearly did not want to answer. He held up his hands and said, "Sorry, I can't take any further questions. There's no time." With that he turned and moved quickly down the stairs and out the heavy doors into the waiting limousine. An RCMP car with the four officers in it followed the Prime Minister's as it moved away from the East Block.

Air Force One (Churchill)
1:07 p.m., CDT

Air Force One, with the President at the controls, had slowed down to 250 knots. To the citizens of Churchill, Manitoba, 2,000 feet below, the Boeing 747 appeared to be hovering there like some great goose followed at a respectful distance by a brace of ducks. The new pair of Canadian Armed Forces CF5 fighters trailed the 747 in formation, about four hundred yards behind and a thousand feet above.

The President banked the big bird in a shallow turn to the left. On the approach to Churchill coming in from the south he had passed over the entrance to the harbour, north of the grain elevators, over the Old Fort on the west side of the Churchill River, and then circled so that he could have a good view of the inner harbour. There were no buildings on the west side of the narrow river mouth, but on the east there were the rail marshalling yards and dock facilities with huge cranes. There was still one ship in the port taking on a load of grain, probably the last of the year. The navigation season at Churchill, which had begun at the end of July when the ice broke up, was just about over.

To the south of the dock facilities lay the town of Churchill, and beyond it the single CNR line that led south to Thompson and Winnipeg. To the east of the town was Fort Churchill, a military base and airport during World War II. The airport, which had survived the post-war years, was paved with an east-west runway sufficiently large to take even the 747.

The airport was bustling with activity as the President swung the big plane in a wide arc overhead. Several vehicles were working on the loading of five Hercules aircraft and several other smaller planes. The President said to the captain, "Ever been here before, Mike?"

"No, sir, I haven't."

"Well, let me tell you a little about this place. You can see that the river flows north into Hudson Bay. It's very narrow. The port is right at the river mouth. During spring break-up, the ice which flows down the river piles up against the ice which is blown in from the north, and so Churchill, which was supposed to be a major ocean port for the Provinces of Western Canada, has been restricted to a shipping period of from 50 to 80 days a year, depending on the weather. What's more, the water is so shallow in the port that only ships under 30,000 tons can get in. As a result, Churchill has never really been able to attract much business except the shipping of grain from the Prairies. There are a few ships that move to and from Europe and bring in booze and things like that, but Churchill has been severely hampered by the short shipping season, the shallowness of the harbour, and by the high insurance rates on ships entering Hudson Bay.

"But things are beginning to happen pretty fast here. The Hercs on the ramp there are running drilling rigs straight north into Baker Lake and beyond, and also into the Chesterfield Inlet region, about 350 miles north. There have been three major copper finds and one nickel discovery in the area, and more exploration work is being done. You may have noticed that about 15 miles south there's a bridge under construction. It's a combined railway and motor vehicle bridge, which will make it possible for the

CNR to continue north right up to Chesterfield and Baker Lake. That railway is under construction now and should be ready in the next year. Alongside it there will be a highway.

"The whole thing is built on eskers. They're long beds of gravel that were left behind after the last ice age. They stretch all the way from Churchill straight north."

"Sir, how on earth do you know all that?"

The President chuckled. "Mike, right now it's my business to know. I was here a few years back and had a good look around then, and I made sure I was well briefed before this trip. Before we left, I thought I might take a look at Churchill, and in the next three or four minutes you'll see why. We'll do one more circuit around the town and the airport and then head out due east."

He went on. "The railway and road I told you about are really the beginnings of a transportation and development corridor that'll stretch all the way from here straight north to Resolute and the centre core of the High Arctic Islands. That corridor already exists as far as air transportation is concerned. An enormous amount of machinery and equipment is now moving from Chicago, Detroit, Toronto and Winnipeg straight into Resolute, and a lot of that supply comes into Churchill for transfer into the Baker-Chesterfield Inlet area.

"Just about the time I was here last, the Canadian government had a special committee called the Great Plains Group. They came up with a proposal to build a new deepwater port on the west coast of Hudson Bay to take ice-strengthened ships up to 500,000 tons which could move ore or liquid natural gas and minerals from the High Arctic. Some bright boy on the committee remembered the eskers, and suggested why not take this fantastic supply of gravel and build a causeway from Churchill straight

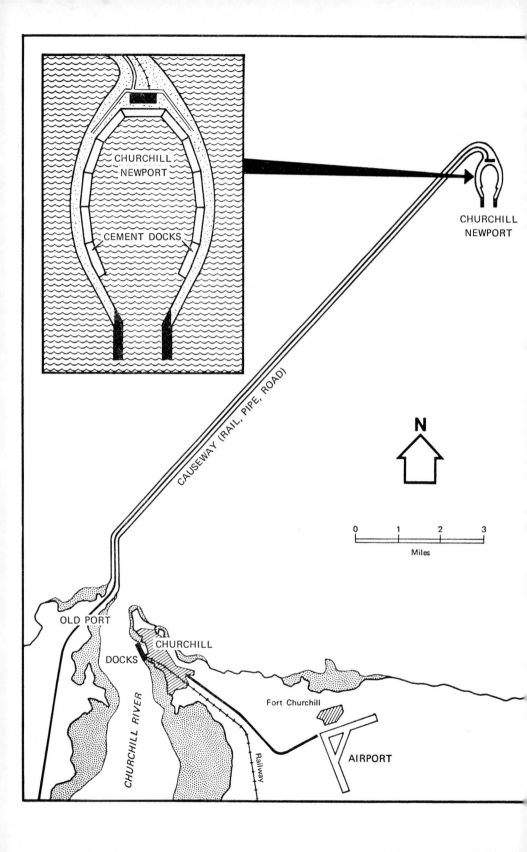

CHURCHILL
NEWPORT

CHURCHILL
NEWPORT

CEMENT DOCKS

CAUSEWAY (RAIL, PIPE, ROAD)

N

0   1   2   3

Miles

OLD PORT

CHURCHILL

DOCKS

CHURCHILL RIVER

Fort Churchill

Railway

AIRPORT

out into Hudson Bay to the point where there is deep water. That's exactly what they've done, Mike. It's about the only imaginative thing the Canadians have done in the North in the last decade."

The 747 was to the east of the airport now, heading north. The President pointed west toward the old harbour and said, "Mike, you see the west side of the old harbour mouth near the Old Fort location? That's where the automated railway and road lead out to the causeway. It goes north about a mile into the bay, turns east-northeast and runs in a straight line for twelve miles. We'll follow it out."

With that the President put the wheel of the 747 gently over to the right, turning the aircraft until it was running parallel to the causeway. The dull gray strip of gravel matched the overcast sky which hung low above the plane.

"There, Mike, you can see the setup now — a three-track railway, a six-lane roadway, and a double pipeline.

"The railway was used to build the causeway. It has an automated loading and off-dumping system that was hooked into the eskers to the west. They moved millions of tons over the period of two years that it took to get the causeway and the basic framework of the port built. We should be able to see the port any minute now."

The captain said, "Mr. President, why are you so interested in looking at this port? Is it of some particular importance to the U.S.?"

"That's a good question, Mike, and the answer is, It sure is. See those pipes on the causeway? One is for crude oil and the other is for natural gas. The southern end of each of those pipes plugs straight into the Chicago-Detroit area. The northern end, just up ahead of us, will plug into crude oil and liquid natural gas tankers coming in from Venezuela, the Middle East and Algeria, as well as from the

High Arctic Islands if the Canadians will get off their butts and give us access."

The captain nodded and pointed straight ahead. "There's the port, sir, at twelve o'clock."

Churchill Newport began to appear out of the haze. From the end of the causeway the port faced south like a huge wishbone. Each arm, like the causeway itself, was a great long pyramid of gravel stretching from its broad base on the floor of the Bay to the surface of the water and then above it to a height of thirty feet above high tide. The top of this great structure, 400 feet wide, carried the road, rail and pipes that had been built for loading and off-loading, and around the entire inner edge were huge docks made of cement which had been floated in and sunk.

The President pointed and said, "Do you see those big cement caissons, Mike? They're built like that because of the ice. If an ice-breaker has to be used to open the port, it could ram its way past those things, and because their walls are sloped rather than vertical, the ice would ride up instead of jamming.

"It's ingenious, isn't it? You have to hand it to them. They've thought it all out. They've even got a system inside that pre-fab port to keep the water from freezing. They drive compressed air through a series of pipes laid under water, and if that's not enough, they pump heated effluent from the town of Churchill to keep the water above freezing point. Between that and the fact that the new port faces south away from the prevailing winds, they should be able to prolong the shipping season well beyond the normal period.

"When you consider all this, you can see why I think this is so important for the United States and why I want to take a good look at it. I can sit on my can in the White House and have people tell me all about it, but I'm the one

90

that has to deal with the energy crisis and I've got to know what I'm talking about."

Col. Wypich nodded in agreement. "I get the picture now, Mr. President, and you're dead right."

"I only wish I'd been able to come up before," the President added. "I would have if I'd been able to shake myself clear. When the native people began blowing up the Mackenzie Valley pipe ten days ago I knew that the time had come to get hold of the situation before it was too late."

He brought the aircraft out of the turn and said to Wypich, "O.K., Mike, if you'll plug in the latitude and longitude of Resolute Bay on the INS and get clearance from Churchill tower I'll set her up for the climb to 40,000 feet, and tell the fighter boys we'll meet them on top."

Leaving a trail of black smoke and diminishing noise, Air Force One climbed sharply and disappeared into low gray cloud just north of Churchill Newport. The faithful Canforce CF5's fell in behind and entered the cloud cover at the same time.

As his driver slowed to pass through the narrow entrance gate of Rideau Hall, the Prime Minister reflected on the close relationship which had existed for many years between the Governor-General and himself. As a law student, Robert Porter had articled in the large Calgary law firm of Simpson and Crane. Alexander Simpson, the senior partner, had taken an immediate liking to the bright, aggressive young man, and the fact that Porter was deeply involved in the work of the same political party that Simpson supported only served to increase his interest. When he was called to the bar after heading his law school class, Bob Porter accepted a generous offer to join the law firm and work with Simpson as his junior. In large measure, he became the son that Alexander Simpson had never had, and during the years in which they worked closely together, the two formed a strong bond of mutual respect which had continued.

On his appointment to the Senate six years after Porter joined the firm, Simpson decided to retire from the practice of law to devote his time to work of the Senate and to the interests of the University of Alberta, of which he had become Chancellor. As well as being a distinguished lawyer, he was known for his deep concern for the cultural, social and physical development of Canada and its people. He had established a Chair of Nationology at the University and gave an annual lecture there on the state of

Canada. This yearly event had become an occasion of major importance in the life of the University.

Soon after entering the Senate Simpson was chosen as its Speaker. His fluency in the French language and his knowledge of French-Canadian culture, combined with a remarkable sense of fair play, and an equitable perception in dealing with the sittings of the Senate, made him universally regarded as one of Canada's most distinguished and respected citizens. He had never fought to uphold the hard party line. In point of fact, he was looked upon by many of his peers as being above politics, but at the same time his allegiance to his party was never in question.

Consequently, when the previous Governor-General, an able French-Canadian, retired from office, Robert Porter's predecessor had reached across party lines and recommended to the Queen the appointment of Senator Simpson. As is the custom, she accepted the Prime Minister's advice and made the appointment, one which was well received throughout Canada, and particularly in the West.

When Alexander Simpson had left the firm to take up his duties in the Senate, Porter decided to make his move into the Northwest Territories. Simpson's work had been in the field of corporation law, chiefly on behalf of the oil and gas firms engaged in exploration and development in Alberta and the Arctic. With the considerable experience he had gained in dealing with these companies and the service firms which supported them, it was not long before Robert Porter's decision to practise in Inuvik, the centre of the oil and gas finds in the Mackenzie Delta, proved to be a rewarding one.

When Bob Porter became Prime Minister, both he and Simpson were delighted to be able to work together again. Porter found the Governor-General unfailingly kind, wise and helpful during the days when he was getting his bearings in office, but never had he needed the counsel and understanding of his old friend more than he did today.

The car swung around the circle in front of Rideau Hall and stopped under the porte-cochere. The Prime Minister got out of the car and acknowledged the salute of the RCMP officer on duty. He mounted the few steps to the front door, which was opened by a young Canadian Forces officer, one of the aides-de-camp to the Governor-General. He said, "I'm Capt. Robillard, sir. His Excellency is expecting you. He's in the drawing room at the end of the hall, if you'd be good enough to follow me."

With the aide leading the way, the two of them left the entrance foyer of Rideau Hall and walked through the reception room and down the long hallway past the formal dining room, reception and writing rooms, to the drawing room which His Excellency used as an office. It was a large, comfortable room lined with bookshelves. At one end there was an ornate, carved stone fireplace, before which a settee and chairs had been placed in a semi-circular arrangement around the coffee table. At the other end, between two windows, there was a beautifully-carved desk at which the Governor-General was sitting.

As the Prime Minister was announced, the Governor-General got up immediately and moved around the desk toward Robert Porter, his hand outstretched in welcome, clear delight and pleasure beaming from his face. He was a man who showed few signs of his age. His piercing eyes and firm chin conveyed strength and authority, and brought warmth and confidence to the Prime Minister. As they shook hands, he said, "I can't tell you how glad I am you're here, sir. If ever I have needed your help and advice it's now."

"Well, Bob, as you know, one of the great delights of my life is to be of service to you. Whether or not I can be in this instance remains to be seen. I'll do what I can, but remember my gratuitous advice is probably worth what you pay for it."

Both men laughed lightly and easily.

The Governor-General took Porter by the arm and said, "Come and sit down over here by the fireplace. I've ordered some tea—or would you prefer a glass of sherry?"

"As a matter of fact, Your Excellency, I would prefer the sherry."

The instructions were given to the aide and the two men sat down, facing each other across the coffee table. The Governor-General leaned back and took out a small cigar. "Well, Bob, I understand we have a crisis on our hands."

"A crisis of the first order, sir. If I may, let me fill you in on everything that has happened and tell you about the plan of action for the rest of today and tomorrow."

The Governor-General nodded his approval and puffed at his cigar.

The Prime Minister began with the telephone call from the President and traced the events and plans through to the point of his proposed discussion with the President the next evening, at which time he would inform him of the decision made by the Canadian Parliament.

The sherry was silently served. The Prime Minister took a sip from time to time as he proceeded. His host sat back and puffed occasionally on the cigar as he listened intently to everything that was being said.

When it was over, the Governor-General slowly shook his head. "Incredible, simply incredible."

Nothing was said for a few moments. Finally His Excellency broke the silence. "You know, Bob, in one way you are in a fortunate position whether you realize it or not. You said you're going to meet with the provincial premiers at six o'clock. Has it struck you that the two main points of the ultimatum come strictly within federal jurisdiction rather than provincial? The first has to do with native rights, an area of responsibility which no province has ever claimed. The second—the demand for Arctic Islands gas—has to do with the Northwest Territories and the Yukon, which are still under direct federal jurisdiction since they have not yet received full provincial status.

"So I think that in regard to the first two points, the Parliament of Canada and you as Prime Minister can speak exclusively and without interference from the provinces.

"On the third matter—the one having to do with granting the Americans free access to any part of Canada to enable them to transport gas from the Arctic Islands— things might be more difficult. If they're talking about a pipeline—and I presume they are—then that pipeline will have to come from the Islands either down the west coast of Hudson Bay and through Manitoba and Ontario into New York State or Michigan. Or it will have to come down across Baffin Island, then across Hudson Strait into the Ungava area of Northern Quebec and on from there. If it is to be a pipeline, can you and Parliament commit the provinces, or do you think you have to get their consent?"

The Prime Minister took his last drop of sherry, put down the glass, and replied, "I hadn't thought of the problem in exactly those terms, but it was in my mind that I would have to have the advice and, if necessary, the consent of the premiers. That's why I asked them to come to Ottawa. The question of jurisdiction will very likely be raised by Quebec and possibly Ontario, but perhaps I should raise the matter with them first."

The Governor-General nodded. "Yes, I think you should."

The Prime Minister went on. "One thing is certain. If

I do have to obtain consent of any one of the provinces, it will have to be from the premier alone. He can check with his cabinet, but there's no way the legislatures could be convened in time to endorse or reject that consent. The whole responsibility for the decision will have to be taken by the individual premier.

"And if any one of them balks, I suppose we—that is, Parliament—will have to override the objection. On the other hand, if Parliament rejects the ultimatum, then the question of provincial consent becomes academic.

"In any event, I don't think the Americans will bring the gas out of the islands by pipe, because I don't think it's technically possible. A consortium called the Polar Gas Study Group has been trying for years to lay pipe between Melville and Byam Martin Islands. They have had one failure after another. I understand they are running a final test now on a new plastic pipe, but I doubt whether it will be successful. It's my guess that they'll choose to take the gas out by air, using the fleet of huge aircraft which Boeing and the American gas companies have been developing."

The Governor-General said, "Oh, yes, the Resources Carrier. That's the plane we initiated some years back and then lost out on."

"That's right, sir. The Americans carried through with the project and the prototype had its maiden flight in Seattle about six weeks ago.

"Panarctic and Tenneco plan to use the aircraft to fly the gas off the Islands if the pipe doesn't work. They would carry it out on relatively short hauls to Ungava in Quebec or Cochrane in Ontario, say, and then feed it into pipelines there for transmission to New York State. Or, on the other hand, they could decide to extend its range and airlift directly to the United States.

"In any event, they're going to use the RCA to haul the oil from the new Melville wells to market."

The Governor-General thought for a moment. "Bob, there's another question that's been going through my mind. What about the formality of my presence at the opening of the emergency session of Parliament tomorrow?"

"I haven't checked with the Speaker yet, but I think your presence will be required. If a Speech from the Throne is necessary, I'll prepare a one-liner for you. I'll confirm it, but I think you should plan to be present."

The Prime Minister went on. "I think I should tell you, in your capacity as Commander-in-Chief of the Armed Forces, that I have asked the Chief of the Defence Staff to alert the entire military establishment with a view to containing any possible outbreaks or demonstrations of anti-Americanism that might occur as a result of the President's ultimatum.

"The CDS tells me there has been a marked escalation in U.S. military flights over Canada since this morning. I'm not really worried about that; it's obviously part of their game plan. What really worries me is what the President can do to us by economic sanctions. The one he has already imposed is serious enough by itself, but when you get down to it, he could practically destroy our economy overnight if he chose to do so. Whether this will be sufficient to persuade Parliament that it should give in is the real question.

"The other side of that question is whether or not Canadians, and in particular the members of the Commons and the Senate, are sufficiently nationalistic to refuse the ultimatum and face the consequences."

"Well, you'll know soon enough," said the Governor-General. "I can certainly understand the Americans' predicament, but I wish they hadn't chosen this big-stick blackmail-type approach. It just isn't in keeping with their traditional way of doing things."

"Perhaps it is consistent if you look at their track record since World War II," said the Prime Minister as he stood up. "Now, sir, if you'll excuse me, I must go to my meeting with the premiers."

The Governor-General also rose, walked around the coffee table, and taking the Prime Minister by the arm, led him toward the door. He said, "Well, Bob, I don't know that I've given you much help during this visit or any advice, for that matter, but maybe I've given you a chance to review the whole situation and perhaps see the implications of the President's actions and your own in a better perspective."

"Yes, I think you're right. It's a great help to me to know that you're here and ready to back me up."

By this time they had reached the entrance foyer of Rideau Hall. The young aide was holding open the door.

The Governor-General turned and faced the Prime Minister, looking him squarely in the eye. "Now remember, Bob, I'm available to you at any time of the day or night. I will do anything I can to help, anything at all."

The Prime Minister turned and went out the door, quickly passing the saluting RCMP officer, and turned to wave to the Governor-General as he got into his car and was gone.

When the Prime Minister arrived back at his office, he found that Senator Thomas had left.

"He didn't feel comfortable in your office, sir, so he went back to his own," Scott explained on the intercom. "He said to call him when you want him."

"O.K. Where are the premiers, Tom? Have they arrived in town yet?"

"They're all here but Post of Nova Scotia. He's somewhere in Europe and they can't find him, so Margaret Cameron, the acting premier, has come in his place. I've booked them all in at the Chateau Laurier. They'll be here at six. I've set up the Cabinet Room for you.

"And whether you like it or not, sir, I have arranged for steak to be brought in at seven. I know that you will want to get right on to the final preparation of the nine o'clock statement. Do you think you'll be through with your meeting with the premiers by that time?"

"Yes, I must be clear by then. If the meeting hasn't broken up, come in and get me. Say another emergency has arisen so that I can wrap it up. Arrange for some food for yourself; then the three of us can have a bite to eat together and you can bring us up to date on what has been going on.

"After that, we can go over Senator Thomas' draft. Have my secretary stand by to retype as we put on the finishing touches. Would you remind her to use the extra-large type so that I can read the speech without my glasses?"

Tom Scott laughed. "I'll tell her, sir. I don't think she would ever forget, though."

"Have there been any urgent calls?"

"No, none that are really urgent. I've had several calls from your ministers and a lot of other people, but there have been no direct calls for you. I think people realize the importance of the situation and don't want to bother you."

"Good. I'm going to take the next few hours to make some notes about what I want to say in the House tomorrow.

"By the way, have you heard anything from the Minister of Justice about the draft resolution? We should have that by now."

"It's just arrived on my desk this moment. Shall I bring it in?"

"Yes, please do."

By six o'clock the Prime Minister had gone back and forth over the draft motion and made a few minor changes. He called in Tom Scott. "Here's the motion, Tom. I'm satisfied that it's in acceptable form now. Would you please have it retyped and deliver it back to the Minister of Justice as quickly as possible. He's going to circulate it to the other Cabinet ministers. If they will let him have their comments by nine o'clock tonight, he should be able to give me a final draft by 9:30. It might be a good idea if he sent a copy to the party leaders at the same time so that we can arrange a meeting if they have any objections."

"Will do, sir."

The Prime Minister stood up. He looked pale and tired. Scott said, "You've been under a terrible strain today, sir. Are you going to be able to get some sleep tonight?"

"I'll try, but it will have to be here in this office. I want to be near the hot line and close at hand in case I'm needed."

The Prime Minister glanced at his watch. "Good Lord, I'm five minutes late for the meeting with the premiers. They're a sensitive bunch at the best of times, so I'd better get going. Remember to come and get me, Tom, if the meeting hasn't broken up by seven."

After leaving Churchill, Air Force One climbed back up to 40,000 feet. The President levelled it off and turned the controls over to the pilot, then went down to the office to be briefed on events as they were happening in Ottawa. He scanned the summary of the Prime Minister's remarks made in response to his own, snorted a couple of times, and said to Wolf and Johnston, "Well, you've got to give that young fellow credit. He's certainly trying hard."

They had reached the south end of the Boothia Peninsula and were starting down. The cloud cover below had disappeared and they were able to see the vast reaches of the Canadian Arctic eastward to Baffin Island and westward towards Victoria and Banks Island. Stretching out in front of them was the great channel which separated the mainland from the Arctic Islands — the historic Northwest Passage.

The President pointed out the channel and said, "I came up here to see the *Manhattan* sail past Resolute Bay in September '69 with a group of people from Montreal who were making the trip at the invitation of Nordair.

"We found her to the west of Resolute Bay, steaming through a great pan of ice. She was a pretty sight, looked right at home in that setting, but the Canadians weren't very happy that she was here. She represented a threat to their claim that the waters of the Northwest Passage belonged to them. They've passed all sorts of legislation since, claiming sovereignty, which they can't possibly enforce, but the voyage gave notice that we intend to back up our position that the Passage is high seas."

Soon Air Force One came in for a landing on the new 10,000-foot runway at Resolute Bay. In the years since his last trip, only the centre core of Resolute had changed appreciably. The single-storey, red-coloured prefabricated buildings that had been brought in by ship to serve as offices, hotel, and administrative buildings were still there, but there was now also a high-rise building like the one in Frobisher. And there were several new hangars lying to the west of the runway, and a great many more fuel-storage tanks.

Resolute Bay had become, in fact, an Arctic boom town. Though it was a poor airport because of uncertain weather conditions, it made an excellent naval base, and had developed into the major regional centre serving the growing gas and oil developments in the Sverdrup Islands. The recent discovery of a massive pool of oil on Melville Island had added to the already enormous discoveries of gas on the Sabine Peninsula and on King Christian, Ellef Ringnes, Thor, Axel Heiberg, and Ellesmere Islands. The number of rigs drilling in the area had increased from thirteen to fifty within a ten-year period. Resolute was for the President just a transfer point, however, the last possible landing space for the giant 747 in that part of the world. With no more than a quick look around to survey the changes which had come about since he was there before, the President went aboard the Hercules transport that was ready and waiting for him. Wolf and Johnston and the rest of the staff would remain on Air Force One to provide the link between the President and the outside world.

The Canadian fighter planes, the fifth pair to join them,

scrambled to refuel and took off shortly after the President. It was by then four o'clock in the afternoon local time, but the sun was still high in the sky. The weather was "ceiling and visibility unlimited." The Herc flew low at 2,000 feet so that the President could clearly see the geological formations, especially the huge salt domes which dotted the islands from Melville to Ellesmere. It was at the edge of these domes that the oil and gas finds were occurring with such remarkable frequency.

They had taken off in a northerly direction, but at Bathurst Island they turned left to swing over the Magnetic North Pole and then due west toward Melville Island. The President wanted to take a look at the main base of Panarctic at Rea Point and at the work going on at Drake Point and Hecla, where development wells were now being drilled.

When they reached Drake Point the President said, "Circle around, Captain. I want to have another look. It was right about here that the first big gas discovery was made in January '70. It came up under such enormous pressure that it blew. It took several months before they could bring it under control. The same sort of thing happened elsewhere in the Arctic, too. No one had the know-how or the technology then to cope with high-pressure finds like that.

"Well, I guess I've seen all I need. We can head south now."

As the captain lined up for the final approach to the Polar Gas base, the President said, "Are you going to land on the ice?"

The captain nodded, "Yes, sir. I checked it out when we were on our way across from Fairbanks earlier today. The strip is serviceable, the ice moves and opens up a bit here and there in August and September, but with freeze-up on it's real solid and no problem."

When they had landed and had taxied up to the cluster of four shacks which served the airstrip, the captain said, "You could probably communicate directly with Air Force One using the base camp radio, sir, but we should really be the master ground net because of the extra communications we have on board. They give us more flexibility."

"Fine," said the President. "Bear in mind that I may want to get the hell out of here fast if something big comes up." He unstrapped his seat-belt and with the help of the navigator, put on his army parka. He hoisted himself down a ladder to the cargo deck and moved quickly toward the passenger door on the port side of the aircraft. The crew chief had put down the steps by the time he reached the door.

As the President stepped out of the aircraft he was hit by a blast of freezing air whipped up by the propellers, which were still turning. He ran quickly to get out of the propwash toward a tall figure, dressed in muskrat parka and mitts, caribou mukluks and heavy dark trousers, waiting to meet him.

"Welcome to Polar Gas, Mr. President," the man said. "I'm Harold Magnusson. I'm with Tenneco out of Houston, assigned to Polar Gas Study as Chief Engineer, trying to pick up the pieces here."

"Mighty proud to meet you, son. Glad to find a fellow Texan, even in these parts."

They walked toward the Polar Gas helicopter, which started up as they approached. When they had climbed in, Magnusson said, "What I'd like to do, sir, is take you to the base camp, show you a model of the under-water pipeline we've been working on, explain the system, and brief you on the test we're running tomorrow morning."

The President said, "That sounds fine, Harold. I'd like

105

to hear and see as much as I can while I'm here." He turned to look at Magnusson and smiled. "I bet you could even find a big Texas steak in the freezer if you looked."

"I wouldn't be at all surprised, Mr. President. We're real proud to have you here as our guest. This is a big event for us at Polar Gas. We have a visit from the President, and we've finally got the line installed under the ice in a new system that I've put together in the last year and a half. We were going to run the first test this morning, but when we got word that you were coming, we put it off until early tomorrow morning so you could see it."

The President turned to Magnusson and said, "Son, let me tell you something. For the last four years I've been watching the work at this station with an eagle eye. I've heard about every failure and every disaster. I've also heard a lot about you since you got here, and they tell me if anybody can make this thing work you can. I knew you were going to be running the experiment, and that's what helped me make the decision to come up here. The success or failure of this test is of tremendous importance to us. If it fails, I don't think we've a hope in hell of licking this energy crisis. If it succeeds, we've got a real fighting chance. So I'm mighty pleased, Harold, that you waited until I got here."

Ottawa / 6:50 p.m., EDT

The Prime Minister glanced at his watch. He would have to wind up his meeting with the premiers soon, and they certainly weren't making much progress.

From the moment Porter had finished his report on the emergency, the discussion had been hot and heavy, and the premiers were still arguing, pounding the table and shouting at each other when their local interests clashed.

As never before, the Prime Minister could see the weakness of Canada's constitution, created in 1867. Regional differences had been strong then, too, and the provinces which had joined together to form Canada had seen to it that under the terms of Confederation they would retain much of the legislative authority, particularly over the natural resources within their own boundaries.

Under the American federal system, the powers of the states had been made secondary to the power of the Congress in all areas of national interest. Thus the President could deal from strength in this war of intimidation, while the Prime Minister had the difficult job of bringing the premiers to a consensus in support of his position.

Robert Porter was tired. Time was running out. He had to rally his strength and bring the meeting to a conclusion. In a firm voice he broke into the heated discussion. "Miss Cameron, gentlemen! I wonder if I might attempt to sum up where we stand. It's nearly seven o'clock. Most of you have travelled a long way today under trying circumstances. I'm sure you'd like to have dinner, talk with your people back home, and get ready for the briefing tomorrow morning.

"I've given you the wording of the resolution to be presented in the House formally tomorrow. Listening to your remarks, it seems, at the moment at least, that five of you will likely favour accepting the ultimatum and five will be for rejecting it.

"May I suggest that each of you let me have your decision before I rise to conclude the debate in the House tomorrow afternoon so that I will have your viewpoint before me. Arrangements will be made to have your opinions delivered to me. A special section in the Spectators' Gallery opposite my seat will be reserved for you and a page will be assigned to carry your messages."

The Premier of Manitoba, Boris Wegeruk, broke in. "If I give you my opinion on what should be done with the ultimatum, Prime Minister, I'm not sure I want it made public or referred to in the House."

That drew a retort from Stewart Andrews, Premier of Alberta. "Look, if you're going to take a position, take it so that the members of the House and the people of your province know what you're thinking. This is the time to stand up and be counted, Boris!"

The Prime Minister said, "Why don't we leave it this way — if you don't want me to refer to your position in the House, let me know."

Margaret Cameron put it right on the line. She looked at the Prime Minister with animosity, her dark eyes flashing. She was a vital and dynamic woman, intellectually far superior to most in the room. Robert Porter found her stimulating as an adversary as well as tremendously attractive physically.

She said heatedly, "So far as I am concerned, Prime

Minister, and so far as Nova Scotia is concerned, we'll take a stand on this issue and you can let anybody in the world know what our position is. These people"— she waved her hands in a sweeping gesture at Boris Wegeruk —"from the West who are too frightened to tell it like it is are not living up to their responsibilities as Canadians and as leaders in their own provinces.

"For that matter, Prime Minister, you've been hedging on this issue too. Where do you stand?"

The Prime Minister laughed. "You may not agree with me, Margaret, but I've decided to keep an open mind for the moment. I want to hear what you people have to say and what the Cabinet wants to do, and what the people of the country think, before I give my opinion publicly. Obviously I have very strong feelings myself, and I've been under a great deal of pressure from the Cabinet to make my position known even before the debate. But I'm sorry, I simply will not take that approach."

He waited for a biting response, but Margaret Cameron simply shrugged her shoulders, sat back in her chair, and said nothing.

"Now let me see if I can sum up where I think you all stand. Miss Cameron of Nova Scotia, Mr. Renault of New Brunswick, Mr. MacGregor of Prince Edward Island, and Mr. Tallman of Newfoundland are of the view that the American ultimatum should be accepted. They feel that the long history of Maritime connection with the United States has forged a bond that is too strong to be broken. More importantly, the substantially lower level of the economy of their provinces, combined with a widespread feeling that they continue to get the short end of the stick from Ottawa, makes them unwilling to risk the effects of American economic sanctions.

"On the other side of the country, Mr. Ramsay of British

Columbia feels that his province, with its emphasis on resource industries, has had traditionally close ties with Washington and California, its major trading partners to the south, and that it too has been remote from Central Canada and Ottawa. He feels that to attract economic sanctions by telling the Americans they can't have the natural gas to which they feel entitled would be sheer folly.

"Premiers Charbonneau of Quebec and Michael Harvey of Ontario, and the premiers of the other western provinces, Mr. Wegeruk of Manitoba, Mr. Lipson of Saskatchewan, and Mr. Andrews of Alberta, all favour flat rejection of the ultimatum. Indeed, Mr. Andrews of Alberta has put forward the strong recommendation that we should tell the United States that unless the ultimatum is withdrawn we will begin a program of counter-sanctions immediately. Specifically, he proposes that we threaten to cut off our current supply of gas and oil to the United States. In my view, this is an unselfish and statesmanlike proposal. Alberta has by far the biggest stake in this situation. Together with Saskatchewan, they already provide vast quantities of gas and oil to the American market. And yet they are prepared to accept the economic consequences of the counter-sanction."

Andrews, on the Prime Minister's left, broke in. "Prime Minister, what you say is right. We in Alberta have by far the biggest stake in the counter-sanction. If it goes into effect, our market for oil and gas goes right down the drain, and so does our entire provincial economy. But let me tell you that we are Canadians first, and Albertans second. So far as my government and the people of Alberta are concerned, this is a sacrifice we're ready to make."

The Prime Minister paused briefly and then continued. "Well, gentlemen, Miss Cameron, while we seem to be evenly split on the matter of the ultimatum, I take it you are all agreed that we should start to fight back by counter-sanction."

There was a general murmur of assent.

"Very well, then, I'll advise the President immediately."

Consett Head, Melville Island
5:40 p.m., CDT

As they entered the main building of the Polar Gas Study base camp, Magnusson said, "I know there's a lot riding on the test tomorrow. I hope we don't let you down, Mr. President."

Ten members of the staff had gathered in the reception room. After appropriate introductions and a few minutes' conversation, Magnusson said, "Mr. President, I wonder if I might drag you away from these people and show you the model of our system? I've ordered a real Texas steak for you — rare. It should be ready in about fifteen minutes."

"That sounds fine." The President nodded, thanked the group, and accompanied Magnusson down a long hall into a briefing room complete with a blackboard, motion picture and slide projectors. At the front of the room were scale models of the experimental under-water under-ice pipeline crossing. Magnusson said, "Sir, if you'd like to sit on that stool, I'll explain the set-up to you."

The President dutifully perched on the stool next to the models and said, "Harold, what I really need before you start is a large bourbon and soda. It's long past that time of day. I've got to have something to keep the old pump going."

Magnusson ordered two bourbon-and-sodas from the canteen bar and then began.

"Please ask me any questions that come to your mind, Mr. President."

"Sure will."

"The first model is really a vertical view to scale of the crossing that we have to make.

"The line goes from a pumping station here at Consett Head, east across the Byam channel twelve miles to a landfall at May Cove on the west coast of Byam Martin Island. In fact, we've laid two sets of pipe in the water. I'll explain why in a minute. If we're successful, we will put together a system that can pick up all the gas on Melville Island and take it straight across to Resolute on Cornwallis. Then the plan is to hook up with a route to the south. We can go from Resolute across to Devon Island to the east, then across the Northwest Passage to Baffin Island, and then down into Northern Quebec and into New York State. The alternative is from Resolute south across the Northwest Passage to Somerset Island, down the Boothia Peninsula and the west coast of Hudson Bay through Ontario to New York State.

"The reason we started off with our experiment between Melville and Byam Martin is that Melville has a bigger volume of gas than any other island in the Canadian Arctic."

The President said, "Yes, I understand that. I also understand that from 1975 until you came on the scene, several attempts were made to put a metal pipe under the ice, and those experiments were total disasters."

"Yes, sir, that's true. What we have had to do is find a system to put a pipe or a series of pipes under the water deep enough down to be out of reach of the moving ice. There's evidence of ice scouring on the bottom down to depths of 250 feet, and there are pressure ridges which

113

cause formations to a depth of anywhere from thirty to a hundred feet. When we lay pipe under the water we have to do it under the worst conditions in the world. You can get temperatures ranging down to 50° below zero here, and with any kind of a wind the chill factor can go down to 100 or 120 below. Those are temperatures which can kill a man and destroy equipment. Metal becomes brittle, and machinery and pipe can crack and become useless. For a rigid metal pipe, the ice has to be opened in long sections and the pipe has to be contoured exactly to the bottom. It has to be ballasted, not only to get it down as far as we might have to go, which could be up to 2,000 feet in some channel crossings, but because when you get it down there the gas itself has so much lifting power.

"In addition you have to make a trough in the bottom to take the pipe so that if the ice does scrape along the bottom in the shallower areas it won't rip it up.

"There's another problem with metal pipe, too. Once you get it down a thousand or two thousand feet, how do you maintain it? Or if you make a mistake, how do you get it back up again for repair? On top of all that, there are other natural hazards. In some of the channels between the islands there are currents which have to be dealt with above the 600-foot level, and of course you have to do much of your work in total darkness during the dead of winter. There's no sunlight at all here except a bit of twilight around noon. The summer months, July, August and September, are just as bad, because then the ice tends to open, leaving stretches of water. It shifts, but it never goes away.

"So you can see that putting a pipeline beneath the ice is a hundred times more difficult than laying pipe across tundra and permafrost. It's little wonder that from the beginning of this research work we've had many failures and no successes."

The President nodded his agreement and took a long sip of his bourbon and soda. Magnusson went on.

"One thing I want to stress, Mr. President, is that no matter what we come up with in an operational under-ice pipe, there's no way that pipe can be used to carry oil. The ecology here is very delicate. Bacteriological activity is virtually non-existent and the amount of wildlife that lives on the ice and in the water is enormous. If we had an oil-spill under the ice, there'd be no way of getting it out. It would be permanent and a total disaster for the eco-system.

"So we're not talking about oil, Mr. President, although there has now been a major oil pool discovered here on Melville. Moving the oil is a job for the big airplane."

The President said, "I agree. We're damn lucky that the Resources Carrier is in prototype and it looks as if it will be ready to go soon. We're going to be able to use it to carry crude oil from Melville to New York State direct. That's the only thing we've been able to get out of the Canadian government in the last four years — consent to take the crude oil from Melville — but it's the gas that's the key."

The President stopped, took a long sip, and said, "But don't let me interrupt, Harold. You have the floor."

"Well, sir, let's look at the next model. It's a working model, because I can move some of the parts as we go along, particularly at the location of the pipe in the water. This is a side view of the channel between Melville and Byam Martin, the 12-mile stretch. It's as much as 750 feet deep in places. At the top of the water is a layer of ice ranging from four to nine feet thick, although there are some pressure ridges as thick as one hundred feet. That's the ice we had to get through in order to get the pipe down.

"Now what I've gone for is the use of a flexible plastic pipe rather than metal. My predecessors — and there were three of them — were locked to the use of metal pipe, rang-

115

ing from a big one 148 inches in diameter to a series of smaller ones in spaghetti form. Apparently they hadn't even thought of the potential of plastic. Certainly they never tried it. In their work the metal became so brittle before it was put into the water that it cracked under the ice. Or, if they could get it down without cracking, the joints broke. They ran into problem after problem. In fact, it got so bad that after the third man quit, the Polar Gas group almost gave up. But by that time they'd sunk about $70-million into the project and didn't want to quit without one more try.

"Now here's a sample of my pipe. The plastic is plain, old-fashioned neoprene. It's enormously flexible and impervious to the cold. It's thick enough to stand a lot of internal pressure, but not strong enough on its own to take the fourteen hundred pounds per square inch that these pipes have to carry in order to get the natural gas through them in volume. So what I've done is to strengthen the outside walls by encasing the tube in a sheath of stainless steel mesh.

"When the pipe is lowered to the operational level of 600 feet below the surface, the plastic will collapse like a tube in a tire, but of course the stainless steel mesh will not. And the steel, being in mesh form, allows the pipe to remain totally flexible, which makes it easier for the divers to handle.

"We have it shipped in here in 50-foot lengths, and we set it in the water in spaghetti fashion, as you can see from the model. We need the capacity of a 48-inch diameter pipe. That's the size they've used for the land pipelines. My plastic pipe is twelve-inch, so we tie sixteen of them together once they're in the water.

"Now we've got a pipe that's flexible enough and can still stand the pressure we have to put through it. But there's one major problem with any pipe under water, and that is the enormous lifting force of the gas inside. What we have to do is to create a ballast system all along the line and tie the pipe to it. Then it gets to be quite a tricky job, because the ballast system has to be capable of letting the pipe up for servicing work and at the same time keeping it under control despite the buoyancy. This is the thing we can't really predict with certainty without a live test, so I've run two lines, using different ballast and control systems, as you can see.

"The first system is really quite simple in principle, and it's the one I hope will work because it's by far the easiest to lay. What it boils down to is a series of enormous cement blocks resting on the bottom and attached to the pipeline by a cable system, running through pulleys at the pipeline and at the block. The end of the cable is held up by a buoy floating just under the ice. We can get at it very easily. The pulleys on the cement blocks have locks on them. To lower the pipe, I can pull up on the cable at the surface, and then when I release the pull the locks operate and the pipe is held in its new position. To raise the pipe, I release the locks with a separate control cable.

"Frankly, I'm concerned about that system. With the currents and other forces operating on the pipe, I'm not sure that it's going to work, so we've designed an alternative system which is more complicated but gives us greater control.

"You can see from the model that the second pipeline is attached to a series of towers every few hundred feet. The towers are approximately 120 feet high, although we've adjusted that in places where the floor of the channel is very uneven. The towers are a little like water-towers. At the top there's a tank which is the key to the whole system. Each tower carries many tons of ballast, and when I lower

117

UNDER WATER TOWER SYSTEMS

1. **FLOTATION TANK SYSTEM**
   ∝) MAIN TANK
   b) FLOTATION PRESSURE CONTROL LINE

2. **GAS PIPE LINE SUPPORTS AND DEVICES**
   ∝) HOUSING SYSTEM
   b) ELECTRONIC SENSING DEVICE
   c) COLUMN
   d) GAS PIPE LINES

3. **LANDERS**
   ∝) COLUMNS
   b) PADS
   c) CONCRETE BALLAST

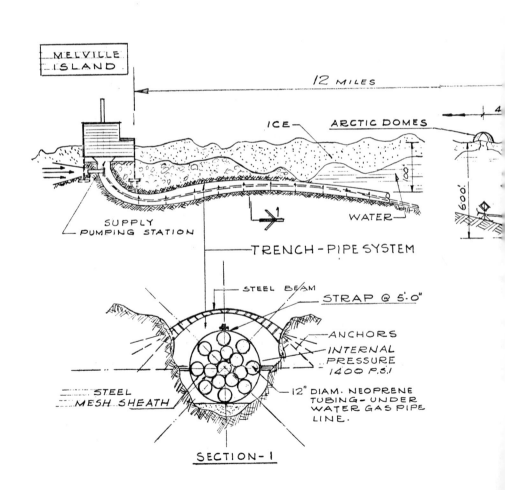

MELVILLE ISLAND

12 MILES

ICE ARCTIC DOMES

SUPPLY PUMPING STATION

WATER

600'

TRENCH - PIPE SYSTEM

STEEL BEAM

STRAP @ 5'-0"

ANCHORS

INTERNAL PRESSURE 1400 P.S.I

STEEL MESH SHEATH

12" DIAM. NEOPRENE TUBING - UNDER WATER GAS PIPE LINE.

SECTION - 1

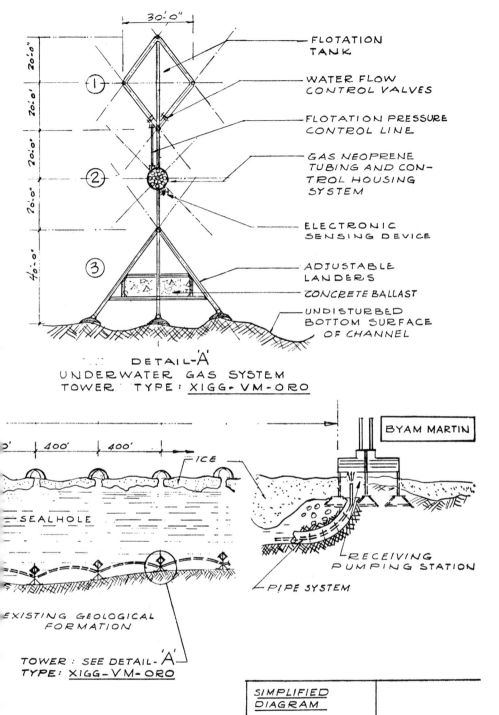

30'-0"

20'-0"
20'-0"
20'-0"
20'-0"
40'-0"

① ② ③

FLOTATION TANK

WATER FLOW CONTROL VALVES

FLOTATION PRESSURE CONTROL LINE

GAS NEOPRENE TUBING AND CONTROL HOUSING SYSTEM

ELECTRONIC SENSING DEVICE

ADJUSTABLE LANDERS

CONCRETE BALLAST

UNDISTURBED BOTTOM SURFACE OF CHANNEL

DETAIL-'A'
UNDERWATER GAS SYSTEM
TOWER TYPE: XIGG-VM-ORO

0'   400'   400'

ICE

BYAM MARTIN

SEALHOLE

RECEIVING PUMPING STATION

PIPE SYSTEM

EXISTING GEOLOGICAL FORMATION

TOWER : SEE DETAIL-'A'
TYPE: XIGG-VM-ORO

SIMPLIFIED DIAGRAM
FOR CONCEPTUAL CONSIDERATION ONLY AND AS APPROVED BY THE ENGINEER.
Γ.Δ.ΞΥΓΚΩΡΟΣ

REGISTERED PROFESSIONAL ENGINEER
G. XIGGOROS
PROVINCE OF ONTARIO

the towers into the water, the tanks are filled with air to provide buoyancy. When the pipeline has been attached to the tower just under the surface and all the towers are hooked on, we lower the whole thing at once. As I indicted, in the Byam Martin Channel the deepest point is about 750 feet. Once the system is resting on the bottom, we flood the tanks on the towers and let the ballast take effect. It's really just like a submarine. When I want to raise the pipeline, I can open valves from the line into the tanks on each tower, blow the water out, and make the system sufficiently buoyant to come to the surface.

"Both the tower system and the cement block system have control valves along the pipeline, of course, so that in case of a break we can shut the flow of gas off instantly and bring the pipeline to the surface for repairs.

"Near the shoreline we have to be very careful because of ice scouring. We lay the pipe in a trench which we dig, using an automated dredge called The Crab, which can crawl along the bottom."

The President shook his head in disbelief. "Son, I've got to hand it to you." He finished off his bourbon and soda and asked, "How do you get the pipes put together and into the water?"

Magnusson replied, "We do it this way. Here at Melville we've carried the trench out to a point where the bottom is 200 feet down. Then we've made a series of holes in the ice all the way across to the other side. These sealholes, as we call them, are about 10 feet in diameter. We've set up domes over each one of them which can be heated and keep the surface of the water free of ice for as long as we want. Then we work our way across, feeding sections of the pipe through the sealholes to the divers working underneath. When we get a line completely across, we can then attach the next 12-inch section, and so on, until we build up the sixteen pipes we need in each line.

"Both pipeline systems are complete now and in position. The pipes are presently filled with seawater. When we're ready to go with the experiment, we'll put a plug of oil through to clean out the water. It will be blown from the Melville side straight across to the Byam Martin end, and out behind the water it's shoving through. Behind the plug will come the gas which we'll take up to operating pressure of 1400 pounds per square inch."

The President broke in. "By the way, Harold, I've got to be out of here as quickly as possible when the experiment is finished. It want to be back in Resolute airborne by 8:15."

"No problem there, Mr. President. We'll get up shortly after five and be out to the main dome at the centre of the channel by six. We're due to start to bring the line under pressure at 6:10, and we should know by 6:30 how things are going to go."

"That's fine, Harold, just great," said the President. "You know, this is a fantastic effort. You've come up with a really ingenious arrangement. I'm looking forward to seeing how it goes tomorrow."

"Well, Mr. President, we'll be able to see, all right. I've got a television rig set up at the main sealhole and lighting down to pipe level, 600 feet, so that we can watch as the pressure is applied. And of course we've got all sorts of sensors set along the pipe to check on the effects as the pressure builds up."

The President slid off his perch, straightened up, and said, "Son, I think you'd better let me at that steak. I'm starved."

As the two men moved toward the door the telephone

rang. Magnusson answered and then turned the phone over to the President. "It's for you. Mr. Wolf calling from the 747."

The President took the phone and said, "Yes, Irving."

Wolf's voice came back. "Prime Minister Porter has been trying to reach you, Mr. President."

"Well, I can't talk to him right now, Irving. We're just going to eat. Let his people know that I'll be available at 7:45, that's 8:45 their time. I'll be in touch with you then. O.K.?"

"I'll pass the word, Mr. President."

"By the way, Irving, the experiment that I want to see will take place here tomorrow morning shortly after six, so I'll get back to Resolute by 7:45 and we can be out of there immediately."

"I'll tell Wypich, Mr. President. We'll be set to go as soon as you get here."

Robert Porter was back in his office, eating the steak Scott had produced and working on the draft of the TV address for nine o'clock. He had discussed the counter-sanction with both John Thomas and Scott, with Michael Clarkson, the Minister of Finance, and finally had reviewed it carefully with the Governor-General. They had all agreed that cutting off the oil and gas supply to the United States was a powerful weapon which stood a good chance of forcing the President's hand and making him lift the ultimatum.

At 7:45 a call was placed to the President. The two exchanged terse greetings, and the President said, "Well, what can I do for you?"

"Mr. President, you've hit Canada hard today, first with your ultimatum and then with the decision to cut off the flow of investment capital even before we had a chance to respond."

"Yes, it was a little rough, but I want to let you people know I mean business."

"We already knew that. It takes a lot to get Canadians excited, but I think you've certainly been able to do it today. Now Mr. President, let me put it to you straight. We are by no means as helpless in this country to resist blackmail as you think. As the United States' largest trading partner, we have very powerful economic weapons of our own, and since you have chosen to invoke sanctions against us without any prior discussion or warning, I am now going to give you a counter-sanction. But I intend to be fair about it; I won't impose the sanction if you agree to the condition I suggest."

"Well, let's hear it."

"Your country is currently receiving about 1½-million barrels of oil and three-billion cubic feet of gas per day from Western Canada. While Montreal and the Maritime Provinces used to be dependent upon oil supply from the United States, they too have a direct pipeline connection now with the West. Therefore, I'm going to order the flow of Canadian oil and gas into the United States cut off immediately unless you agree to lift the ultimatum."

There was silence for a few moments. Then Porter could hear the President chuckling. "You know, down in Texas we like cool poker players, and you do pretty well, young fellow. That's a pretty good card you've played, but not quite good enough. I'll tell you what I'll do. If you agree not to impose the counter-sanction, I'll agree to lift the embargo I put on at noon and not to put on the further sanction I was going to impose at midnight. In fact, I agree not to order any other sanctions between now and six o'clock tomorrow evening. The midnight sanction, by the way, was to close the border to the movement of all goods."

It was Porter's turn to pause as he thought over the President's move. Reluctantly he said, "I'm afraid you won that hand, Mr. President, but if nothing else, I think you've got the message that we have some weapons of our own."

"Yes," the President replied, "but I think you'll find you're outgunned. Is there anything else, Mr. Prime Minister?"

"No, that's all for the moment. You'll hear from me."

"I'm sure I will." The President hung up, while Porter muttered to himself, "Half a loaf is better than none, I guess."

John Thomas said, "You've got a real tough cookie at the other end of that telephone. He's going to play this one right down to the wire."

Porter nodded. "Yes, you're certainly right. But now I've got to get that speech finished. Let's go over it once again."

Inuvik / 6:30 p.m., CDT

Freddie Armstrong picked up the mike in the single engine Otter and said, "Inuvik Tower, this is Romeo November Echo, 10 miles northwest at 3,000 feet VFR from Aklavik, landing at the town strip. Over."

"RNE. This is Inuvik Tower. You are cleared to the town strip. The wind is 330 at five. The altimeter setting is 3019. I have no other local traffic in the area."

"Roger, Tower. Will you please close my flight plan?"

"Roger, wilco."

Freddie put the VHF mike back on its holder. It was dark now, and he peered ahead into the twinkling lights of Inuvik for his marker, the wafting white plume of the steam from the power plant. He would turn left over the power plant on his final leg inbound to the airstrip northwest of the town along the west arm of the Mackenzie.

Freddie Armstrong was a living legend in the Arctic. An Indian who had competed successfully in a white man's field, he had graduated from high school, saved his money, and gone outside to Edmonton to take flying lessons. Back in Inuvik he had worked hard to save enough money to buy his own airplane, a Cessna, had obtained a Class 4 charter licence and started to work to build up his firm, Caribou Air Services Limited, at a time when no other operators were in the area and nobody gave a damn about the prospects of Inuvik or oil or gas in the Mackenzie Delta. The discoveries in the North brought so much business that he had been able to enlarge his fleet to ten aircraft, but they had also brought increased competition, and the Air Transport Committee in Ottawa had granted charter licences freely to the well-financed carriers from the south who soon moved in with their Twin Engine Otters and other sophisticated machines.

On top of that, his crews had cracked up two of his larger aircraft just as things were reaching their peak, and this financial setback had almost put him out of business.

But Freddie Armstrong was a determined man. He stuck to his guns and now had a reputation, all through the Arctic, as someone who really knew his job.

He glanced over at Sam Allen in the right-hand cockpit seat and thought, not for the first time, that Sam was a heck of a nice guy. He was glad he'd been able to do him a favour. Funny, though, that Sam and Bessie didn't have any pelts with them. When he dropped them off about twenty miles west of Aklavik the morning before, Sam had told him that they were going out to look after some muskrat traps set by Sam's brother Pete, who was sick in Aklavik. So he'd expected them to have at least two dozen skins when he picked them up. He asked Sam if they'd got any rats. And Sam replied, "Sure did, Freddie, got plenty, but I bagged them and hung them off the ground in a tree just north of Rat River, so Pete can pick them up there as soon as he's better."

Freddie saw that Sam's harness was done up, and turned back to check on Bessie. She was sitting in the passenger compartment on the right of the aircraft, and at his glance nodded and pointed to the harness. Freddie lined up on the runway lights and decided he'd do a full-flap landing because there was no wind. He pumped the flaps down and the nose of the aircraft came down in response. He checked his air speed, cutting back to 58 knots. He cranked on a bit more power to get ready for the roundout which was fast approaching, and as he passed the end of the airstrip, pulled back on the throttle and the wheel. The aircraft rotated beautifully and sank gently onto the snow. The skis squeaked and squealed as the plane slowed abruptly. A short landing was a trademark of the old Otter, and Freddie Armstrong was still one of the best pilots in the business.

Freddie cranked up the flaps and made a wide, sweeping turn into the dispersal area on the east side of the town strip. "Well, Sam, another successful non-crash."

Sam smiled, "Beautiful landing, Freddie, just great."

As they unstrapped and began to get ready to move out of the aircraft, there was a sudden pounding at the rear right-hand door. It was jerked open from the outside. Sam looked back into the ruddy, black-moustached face of Staff Sergeant Ray of the Inuvik detachment of the RCMP. Fear gripped him. He glanced quickly over at Bessie. Her eyes were wide with fright. Ray clambered up into the cabin next to Bessie and stopped, his hand on the green knapsack which contained a spare explosive charge, a timer and arming mechanism Sam had brought back with him. He said, "Sam, we've been looking all over for you. The Prime Minister has been trying to get hold of you all day. They tell me it's really urgent."

Sam moved quickly to get out of the Otter. As he passed by Bessie, who was still strapped in her seat, he said, "I'll take the knapsack with me, Bessie, if you and Freddie can bring the rest of the stuff." He followed Staff Sergeant Ray out the door, jumped down onto the snow, pulled up his parka around his head, and strode rapidly toward the shack Caribou Air Services called its office. Parts and pieces of aircraft were strewn about the area. Freddie's mechanics had to do a lot of their work outside now, since their original hangar had been sold to keep the business going. When they entered the office the Sergeant went immediately to the desk and handed a strip of paper to Sam.

"Here's the number. The Prime Minister's secretary said that he would probably be at a meeting when you called, but he gave her instructions to get him out. It sounds to me as though it's pretty important."

Sam asked, "Did she say why he was calling?"

"No. I asked if there was a message, but all she would tell me was that it was urgent to find you as soon as possible. Apparently they called your house, the Eskimo Inn, your office, and, from what I can gather, two or three other places in town. I guess your office told them you were out in the bush trapping."

Sam picked up the phone and was soon through to the Prime Minister's secretary. She said, "Oh, Mr. Allen, the Prime Minister will be very pleased we've finally got you. He's just finishing the meeting. If you'll hang on for a minute, I'll let him know you're on the line."

As he waited for the Prime Minister, Sam looked out into the darkness toward the aircraft where he could see Bessie and Freddie unloading the tent, the portable stove and sleeping bags. As they reached the office, Porter came on the line. "Sam, how are you? I haven't talked to you for a long time."

Sam shifted from one foot to the other and said, "Hi, Bob — I mean, Prime Minister. I'm fine. How does it feel to be the Chief?"

"Well, being the Chief is sometimes good and sometimes bad. Today's a bad day, Sam. I need your help, and I need it fast. I haven't time to give you all the details, but the President of the United States has dumped a real problem in my lap. He's given Canada an ultimatum. We have to

129

agree to let the U.S. have all the gas it wants from the Arctic, and we have to give the Americans free access to the area so that they can get it out. On top of that, we have to guarantee to settle with the native people in the Northwest Territories and the Yukon immediately to get the bombings stopped. As you know probably better than anyone, I want to see us make a proper arrangement on native rights, and I've been trying to make plans for serious discussions, but with the pressure of everything else in Ottawa since I became Prime Minister I couldn't move as quickly as I wanted."

Sam broke in, "Yes, I know, Bob. The Indian Brotherhood and our organization and everybody else up here has been getting pretty uptight because nothing's been going on, and the pipeline's just about finished."

"Yes, I know. That's the problem. I don't know who's doing the bombing, and I don't suppose you do either, but I imagine you can find out if you have to, since you're the head man in the Mackenzie area. Somehow I've got to get a message to those people and let them know that we're in a crisis and it's imperative that they stop the sabotage immediately.

"I want you to pass the word along that if the native people are really interested in having a settlement, then they're going to have to help me maintain the strongest possible bargaining position with the President. The deadline on the ultimatum is six o'clock tomorrow night. The blowing up of the pipe has got to be stopped now. There must be no explosions during that time."

Sam's smile had long since been replaced by a frown of concentration as he sorted out the implications of what the Prime Minister was saying. "Bob," he said, "what if I can't get the message through to the right people? What if there's a blast between now and tomorrow night?"

"I don't know what the consequences will be, Sam, except that they won't be good. You know there are a lot of people in Parliament who don't agree that we should settle with the Indian and Eskimo people. I've got to have your support to get a fair settlement through. I can tell you that it's absolutely crucial to your people that these bombings be stopped."

Sam turned away from the window and sat down on a rickety office chair.

"I'll have to leave that one with you," said the Prime Minister, "and I can't give you much time to do something about it, because I need you here in Ottawa immediately to begin settlement talks. I'll be asking the Minister of Indian Affairs and the Secretary of State to begin meetings with you and the heads of the Yukon and Northwest Territories Indian Brotherhoods starting tomorrow morning. There's an Armed Forces Hercules on its way now to pick you up. It should be there by eleven o'clock your time. Then it will go over to Whitehorse to pick up Chief Abner and back to Yellowknife to pick up the new President of the N.W.T. Indian Brotherhood. What's his name?"

"Peter Firth. He's a Dog Rib Indian."

"Well, Sam, I hope you're prepared to come to Ottawa."

"I sure am, Bob, even though I hate the lousy place. But, look, if I can make contact with the people who've been blowing up the pipe and get them to stop, can I promise them amnesty? Maybe they've already planted some bombs. If so, they'll have to go out and defuse them and perhaps get some help. What if they're caught while they're doing that?"

There was a pause while the Prime Minister considered what Sam had said and the way in which he'd said it. He replied, "You've got a good point. I'll see to it that the Attorney General and the RCMP lay no charges against anyone who co-operates in finding and defusing any explosive charges on the pipeline. In fact I'll see that the RCMP are instructed to do everything they can to assist in getting to the locations and getting the bombs defused."

Sam looked down at his elaborately beaded and embroidered mukluks and said slowly, "Will the amnesty be extended to anyone who has had a part in the blowing up of the pipes to this point?"

The Prime Minister's voice said firmly, "Yes. My secretary's here with me. She's been taking down what I've said about the amnesty and a telegram will go out to you immediately and to the RCMP to confirm."

Sam turned around in his chair to face Ray and said, "Bob, I've got Staff Sergeant Ray of the RCMP here with me. If you'll tell him what you've just told me about the amnesty for everybody, then I think we can get this whole thing going pretty quickly."

"O.K. Put him on."

Sam handed the telephone to Ray, who identified himself and listened quietly to the Prime Minister as he repeated what he had said to Sam. Porter went on, "You people have a Twin Otter up there, haven't you?"

"Yes, sir, we have."

"Well, if Sam puts you in contact with people who know where the bombs are, I suggest you use that plane to get out to the pipe. From what I can gather from Sam, there are bombs there right now. You'll have to act quickly, because the Herc. that's being sent up for Sam and the people from Whitehorse and Yellowknife will be into Inuvik by eleven o'clock tonight."

"We'll do our best, sir."

"Good, now will you put me back to Sam, please?"

Sam took the telephone from the Staff Sergeant and said, "I'll look after everything here, Bob. Now that we've got the amnesty thing going I guess I should tell you it's Bessie and I who've been setting the bombs."

"I had that figured out five minutes ago, Sam."

Staff Sergeant Ray shook his head slowly from side to side, as much in gesture of disappointment as in disgust. In his book Sam and Bessie had committed a serious crime, and he really wouldn't have expected it of them, though he had to admit that if they wanted to draw attention to the wrongs of their people they couldn't have picked a more dramatic way to achieve it.

The telephone discussion with the Prime Minister over, Sam hung up. He turned to Ray and with a small-boy grin on his face said, "Did you have any idea it was us, Jim?"

The Staff Sergeant shifted slightly, pulled at his moustache, and looked uncomfortable. "As a matter of fact, no, Sam. I thought you'd be too smart to do it yourself. I suspected you knew who was doing it, and maybe even you were planning it, but I had nothing to go on. I certainly didn't think it was you and Bessie. But the main thing now is, how the hell are we going to get those bombs defused? You've got to leave almost at once for Ottawa, so someone else is going to have to do the work."

Sam bent down by the desk and picked up the green knapsack. Flipping it open, he took out the explosive charge and timing mechanism. That brought Ray to his feet quickly.

"Where on earth did you get that?" he asked.

Sam laughed and responded, "No names, Jim. Pretty good-looking stuff, isn't it?" He laid the package on the desk.

Ray was astonished. "It sure is."

Sam went on. "Bessie knows exactly where all the bombs are located. You should be able to land the Twin Otter close to all of them. They're at river crossings. The charges are set to go off in a series over the next twelve days. The first one is set for 7:30 tomorrow morning, so you're going to have to get going as soon as it's light."

"I've taken a fair amount of training in explosives," Ray said, "but you're going to have to go through it pretty carefully for me."

Sam explained the working mechanism and timing device, and the sequence of steps to disable it. "If you turn that wheel the wrong way, Jim, you've got four seconds before it blows."

"Four seconds," thought the Staff Sergeant. "With snowshoes on, that won't get you very far."

Ottawa / 9:40 p.m., EDT

The Prime Minister was looking into the baleful, inanimate eye of the television camera focused on him. His half-hour address was almost finished, and had gone well. He had begun with a review of the terms of the ultimatum and described the meetings he had held during the day and the plans for the briefing in the House of Commons the next morning, followed by the full session of Parliament.

Then he had discussed in depth the American energy crisis, explaining why it was natural gas that was the precious commodity for the United States rather than oil. He had spoken with great sympathy and understanding for the American position, and he had renewed his plea for a calm and controlled response to the United States' action rather than the stirring up of anti-American demonstrations. Finally, he spoke forcefully of the decision to resist the sanctions which had been imposed, and reported on the decision to threaten a counter-sanction and the gains which had thus been won. Then he continued:

"The President now knows, and I hope that the American people will shortly know, that Canadians will not meekly give in to threats and intimidation.

"As we move toward the moment of decision when the Commons and the Senate sit tomorrow afternoon, it becomes more and more important to me that some mechanism be established through which as many Canadians as possible can communicate their views on the ultimatum.

"With the co-operation of the Trans Canada Telephone System, the television networks, and all private TV and radio stations across the country, we have set up a system which will enable any of you who wish to let me know directly whether you think Canada should accept or reject the ultimatum. Simply telephone any of the stations broadcasting in your local area. Switchboards are open and staff are ready to receive calls. When you are connected, do not discuss the situation; merely say 'accept' or 'reject' and then hang up. Please get off the line as quickly as possible so that others can have their opinions recorded. And of course I ask you to make only one such call.

"I ask all of the radio, television and news people in the country not to attempt to influence the poll. It would be in the best interests of Canada if the news media devoted their full attention to reporting the facts. In this way, I hope that as many people as possible will have an opportunity to make their opinions known to Parliament.

"The radio and television stations will receive calls until twelve noon tomorrow, Ottawa time. The results will then be tabulated and passed to me in the House at about three o'clock, before the close of debate, and I will be able to advise the House of the result.

"And so I urge every Canadian citizen who can do so to telephone and pass on his opinion about the ultimatum, saying either 'accept' or 'reject'.

"Thank you and good-night."

Day Two

The telephone was ringing. Porter struggled awake and reached out for it, almost rolling off the narrow couch in the process.

It was Tom Scott's voice. "It's seven o'clock, Prime Minister. You asked me to give you a call."

"Thank you, Tom. I'll get going right away."

Still fogged with sleep, the Prime Minister sat up and tried to collect his wits. God, what a night! It was late when he'd got to bed. The television address had taken much longer than he'd expected — almost an hour — and after that there had been several important telephone calls. He had talked with the Canadian Ambassador in Washington, the Canadian High Commissioner in London, whom he had routed out of bed at 3:30 in the morning, and with several of the Cabinet ministers who wanted clarification and direction regarding the morning briefing.

About midnight Tom Scott had poured a drink for Porter, Thomas and himself, and the three of them sat and talked for a while, speculating about what action the United States would take should Parliament refuse the ultimatum. Finally the other two left and Porter had stretched out on the couch, completely exhausted.

He slept fitfully. Twice he was awakened with reports from the Chief of the Defence Staff, and then by a call from George Townsend, Prime Minister of the United Kingdom, which had come through at 4 a.m. Townsend wanted the Prime Minister to know that Great Britain would stand behind Canada whatever the decision on the ultimatum. If it was rejected, the United Kingdom would do its best to support the economic structure of Canada in the face of the sanctions which the United States would undoubtedly impose, and would attempt to give the country preferential treatment in terms of trade. However, because of the tight restrictions imposed by membership in the Common Market, such preferences would have to be limited. But, as much as anything, Townsend wanted to offer his moral support.

Porter thanked him for the encouragement, and the two men went on to an extensive discussion of military support. Certain emergency measures were agreed on.

After speaking to Townsend, the Prime Minister called the Chief of the Defence Staff to inform him of the military arrangements he had made and to give him further instructions.

And now, just as he had got back to sleep, it was time to get going again.

The Prime Minister got up stiffly, showered and dressed quickly in the dark blue suit Mike Cranston had brought in the night before. After that he sat down to the light breakfast that was waiting for him on his desk and opened the Toronto *Globe and Mail*.

He saw at once that the *Globe* had done exactly what he had pleaded with the press not to do. Across the front page was the enormous headline, "U.S. Threatens Canada." Underneath was an editorial by the editor-in-chief and a full report of the ultimatum and the actions of the government. The editorial was strongly anti-American, and called for demonstrations.

Porter was furious. His first thought was to get the publisher and the editor-in-chief on the line and raise hell with them. But he had tangled with both of these men before and he knew that it would be of little value to talk to them. There was never any question that they would change their position, no matter what the facts were, and it was clear to Porter that any call from him would only encourage them to take a more extreme view.

What he did do, however, was to get in touch with his long-time friend, the editor-in-chief of *The Toronto Star* and a bright and dynamic young man who shared many of Porter's views. They discussed the approach the *Globe and Mail* had taken and ways in which the *Star* might treat the situation to counteract the dangerous effect of the morning paper. He also reported on his assessment of feelings of people in the Toronto area, where opinion was running high in favour of rejecting the ultimatum. Anti-Americanism was being expressed everywhere, and parades and demonstrations were already being organized.

At this point, off the record, the Prime Minister said that he had ordered the Chief of the Defence Staff to move regular-force troops into the city during the night. They were now secretly stationed, with their vehicles and equipment, at the Fort York and Moss Park armouries, and also at the Canadian Forces Base at Downsview. The CDS and his staff were in close co-operation with the Metropolitan Toronto Police and the Ontario Provincial Police. Similar action had been taken in Montreal, Windsor, Winnipeg, Calgary, Vancouver and Edmonton. Military forces were available to provide "aid to the civil power" if called upon by the local authorities.

When he had finished his conversation, John Thomas entered the office. He sat and listened while Tom Scott briefed the Prime Minister on the success of the parliamentary airlift and on general editorial reaction in the Canadian and American newspapers.

141

Scott reported that the leaders of the opposition parties had accepted the proposed motion on the ultimatum with only minor revisions. They had also wanted to know when the Prime Minister would have ready the preliminary remarks he would make in introducing the motion in the House.

"That's right!" Porter said. "I promised to let them have a look at what I intended to say in advance. Could you draft out something, John? It should be very brief."

"Glad to. I'll have it for you in fifteen minutes."

Thomas went off to another office to begin work on the draft, and after some more instructions, Tom Scott left the office. The Prime Minister called in his secretary to dictate notes on some of the points he wanted to make in closing the debate in the House.

It was soon time to leave for the Commons Chamber and the briefing. Before leaving, Porter called Scott on the intercom. "Tom, I'm leaving now. Would you hold the fort here and send down messages only if they are of the utmost urgency? The RCMP are standing by to get me through the mob of reporters that I'm sure are just outside the door."

"Yes, sir, they're there, all right, only this time there must be twice as many as yesterday."

"Good Lord!"

Bracing himself, the Prime Minister picked up his black loose-leaf notebook and went out to the reception area to pick up the RCMP escort.

A mob scene it was. Clearly, the emotions aroused by the bluntness of the ultimatum were reaching a high pitch. There was a tremendous milling about and shouting as the reporters attempted to put their questions to him.

The Prime Minister grabbed the sleeve of the RCMP Staff Sergeant, senior man in the group, and shouted something in his ear. The Sergeant disappeared back into the reception room and reappeared immediately with a chair. Porter climbed onto it so that he could look over the crowd and speak. He raised his arms to signal for quiet. Gradually the babble of talk died down.

There was an air of tension and expectancy. This was *the* event and this was the man at the centre.

The Prime Minister smiled as he began to speak. "Good morning, ladies and gentlemen."

There was much clapping and cheering.

"There is very little new for me to report to you this morning. Not a great deal has transpired since my television address last night.

"As you know, an extensive briefing of all the Members of Parliament is to begin in the Commons Chamber in three or four minutes' time. I want that meeting to get under way promptly because there is so much to cover in the three-hour period available.

"The Press Gallery will of course be open during the briefing, and we have arranged for television coverage in the Commons, so the people of Canada will be getting the same information and background as their elected representatives and the Senate. The debate this afternoon will also be televised across the country."

A shouted question. "What position are you going to take on the vote on the ultimatum?" It was the same question he had declined the day before.

"That is not a question I wish to answer at this time. When I come to wind up the debate in the Commons this afternoon I shall make my position absolutely clear. By then, too, we should have the results of the national telephone poll that is now going on. Before I state my position, I want to know what response there has been from the people."

"It's been fantastic," a reporter shouted.

"Good!" said the Prime Minister. "Now if you will all be kind enough to let me and my football team through, I'll get the briefing under way."

The crowd of reporters opened up easily to let Robert Porter and his escort through. When they reached the foyer to the House of Commons the Prime Minister left the escort behind and proceeded directly into the government lobby. It was crowded with members of his party hurrying to their seats. Porter acknowledged the greetings as he walked down the long room towards the curtained entrance to the aisle which led directly to his place on the front bench.

As the curtain fell behind him and he started down the incline of steps towards his seat, he was startled by a thundering noise, a tremendous pounding of the desks by members of every party and a burst of applause from the galleries and from the senators seated on the floor of the House. It was an unusual sound, and the Prime Minister was profoundly moved by it.

As he walked slowly down the steps toward his seat, his eyes swept across the vast chamber from left to right. They took in an impressive and most unusual sight, one that he would never forget. Nor would he forget the atmosphere of apprehension and excitement that would inevitably mount as the events of that day moved inexorably forward, building up wave upon wave to the crest of decision which was to come shortly after five o'clock.

He stopped halfway down the aisle to acknowledge the rare tribute being paid to him. He knew that actually the applause was not for him but for the position he held as the First Minister of Canada. Nevertheless, he was deeply impressed by this sign that all present were united in a strong feeling for their country.

He turned to the left and saw the faces of his own members, sitting at their seats thumping away vigorously. He could see the vacant Speaker's Chair, that small elegant throne from which the "chairman" of Parliament presided over the battles and debates, an ornate, carved dais which the Speaker would ascend that afternoon after the Speech from the Throne had been read in the Senate Chamber.

Overhead, the Press Gallery was crowded with the men and women who reported to the nation the happenings in the House. In the Visitors' Gallery immediately opposite were many familiar faces — ambassadors, friends — and in a special section the provincial premiers, together with the two Commissioners of the territories, Jones of the Yukon and Nellie Vladm of the Northwest Territories.

The Spectators' Gallery was jammed. Everyone who could possibly be squeezed in was there. There were even people sitting in the aisles. At the opposite end of the chamber, two television cameras which were now fixtures in the Commons Chamber, were trained on him.

This was Canada. Canada was in this room, and the eyes of all Canadians were upon Parliament and upon him.

As he resumed his walk down the aisle to his seat, he reminded himself that this was not a session of Parliament but only a briefing. Informality would have to prevail. The Speaker would not be in the chair. He himself would be chairman and general controller of the session.

In front of the Speaker's Chair a large projection screen had been placed. To the left of the screen was a long table on which sat a lectern with a set of microphones mounted on it. The Prime Minister could see the Minister for External Affairs, his deputy and two other staff members seated at the table, ready to begin the briefing.

The Prime Minister arrived at his seat and remained

standing. He nodded and half bowed to the Leader of the Opposition and to all sides of the House, while the banging of desks and applause kept on. Finally, with a gesture he had had to use twice with the press in the last few hours, he raised his hands to ask that the meeting might come to order and the proceedings begin.

As the din began to subside, he took out his glasses and ran his eyes over the points he had prepared in his notebook.

The Chamber had fallen silent. There was the odd cough and clearing of throat here and there and some activity in the Press Gallery. As the Prime Minister began to speak, even the small noises died down and his voice filled the vast chamber.

"Ladies and gentlemen," he began, "we are at the opening of what may well be the most important and momentous day of decision in the history of Canada."

The Polar Gas helicopter levelled off at two hundred feet as it moved away from the base camp bound for the main dome in mid-channel between Melville and Byam Martin Islands. Across the twelve-mile stretch of snow, bathed in the Arctic dawn sunlight, the President could make out patches of turquoise-coloured ice — pure, hard, deep ice. Stretched out across the channel like beads on an invisible thread were the beet-red domes that covered each of the sealhole stations over the pipelines.

Magnusson, sitting behind the President, tapped him on the shoulder and pointed to the right. "That's the pumping station, sir. The compressors will start at 6:10 sharp. We'll be at the master sealhole in about three minutes, about two minutes after six, which will give us just enough time."

Ahead of the aircraft the President saw the broad sweep of Byam Martin Island, a brownish, treeless tundra, rising to heights above the level of the swift-moving helicopter. Then out to his right beyond the southern tips of both Melville and Byam Martin, the broad expanse of whiteness disappeared into the horizon. High above, his eye caught the vapour trail of a high-flying jet leaving its impermanent white mark on the crystal blue of the cloudless Arctic sky.

The President turned to Magnusson and asked above the

noise of the helicopter, "Get any polar bears in these parts?"

"Sure do, Mr. President. We don't let our people get away from the domes on the ice any distance at all. The bears are mean creatures and, man, are they fast! Had a fellow killed over at Panarctic's base camp last year, so we treat them with great respect."

The helicopter pilot set the small machine down gently just a few feet from the red dome of the master sealhole and cut off his power. He would wait to fly the President back to the Polar Gas base camp and the Hercules transport which would take him to Resolute.

The President and Magnusson entered the dome through the entrance chamber which trapped the cold air like an igloo and then through another door into the dome itself. In the centre was the 10-foot wide sealhole that Magnusson had described to him, the water sitting just about two feet below the level of the ice. The ice surface inside the dome had been covered with plastic material to give a secure footing and also to minimize the heating required to maintain the interior of the dome at an acceptable working temperature of 60°.

In the sealhole a ladder had been attached to the lip of the ice so the divers could get in and out of the water. Mounted on a double A-frame rig directly over the hole was a cable drum carrying the cables from the television sets and pressure gauges mounted on the main control console to the cameras and sensors underwater. One of Magnusson's men was at the pressure gauges checking them for readings prior to the start-up of pressurization. Magnusson introduced him to the President.

Near the sealhole was a rack from which two heavily-insulated diving wetsuits hung. Oxygen tanks, masks,

148

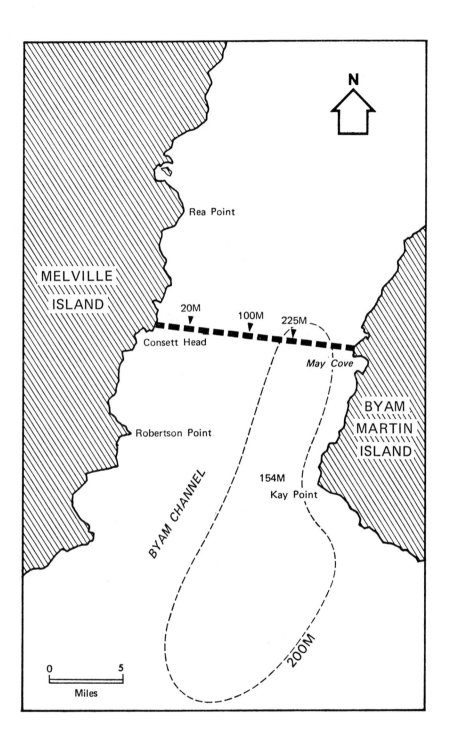

N

MELVILLE
ISLAND

Rea Point

20M   100M   225M

Consett Head

May Cove

BYAM
MARTIN
ISLAND

Robertson Point

BYAM CHANNEL

154M
Kay Point

200M

0   5

Miles

flippers and gloves were neatly piled on the floor next to the rack.

The interior of the dome was bathed in a soft white light from the brilliant, rapidly rising sun, which filtered through two opaque panels in the centre of the dome.

Magnusson moved toward the hole, and the President followed him. They stood at the edge and looked down into the water.

"Because of the possibility one of the pipelines may fail, we've put this dome about a quarter of a mile away," Magnusson said. "The ice here is about eight feet thick. You can see down quite a distance because the water's perfectly clear and the ice lets a good deal of sunlight through. Just below the level of the ice you can see one of the control buoys for the television cable. We've run the cable just under the ice from here across to a point just above the pipes, then down to pipe level. Our divers have been checking the cable buoys and the control buoys for the tower system. In fact, you can just see one of the divers checking the cable buoy immediately under this hole. We also supply power from here to lights down at pipe level for the divers and the TV cameras. We get our electricity from portable generators. You can hear the one for this sealhole chugging away outside."

Magnusson and the President moved to the television sets and the pressure gauges. Magnusson said to the technician, "How does it look, Oscar?"

"Everything checks O.K., Harold. The TV sets and cameras and everything are functioning well, as you can see from the pictures on the screens."

The wide angle television cameras had been lowered until each was directly opposite the pipelines at mid-point of the twenty-yard distance between the two systems.

A 30-foot section of the "tower" pipeline was displayed

on the left screen in colour. The right screen showed the "concrete" system.

The President said, "The insides of the pipes look as though they're squashed."

Magnusson responded, "They are, Mr. President. At a depth of 600 feet the water pressure — about 290 pounds per square inch — is sufficient to cause the neoprene pipe to collapse. The steel mesh sheath retains its shape. When the pressure is applied internally and the gas is fed in, the pipe will come out to its normal shape."

He picked up the small phone on the console. "Compressor Station!"

A voice came back, "Go ahead, Harold."

"Bill, have you confirmation that the checks have been done on all the buoys?"

"Yeah, everybody has reported in that everything is O.K. — that is, everybody except Joe Henderson, who should be at your sealhole."

Magnusson turned toward the sealhole and the sound of splashing. He replied, "Just a minute. He's coming out of the hole now."

A black figure emerged from the water and climbed up the ladder. The diver turned toward Magnusson and gave him a thumbs-up sign. Magnusson continued: "Everything's O.K. here, so we're all set to go. Have you confirmed that the valves at the Byam Martin end are open for the blowout of water and set to shut off external venting when the water and the oil plugs have gone through?"

"I have."

Magnusson said, "O.K., Bill. Turn her on and keep your fingers crossed."

Henderson, the diver, had taken off his wet suit and put on his parka. He was introduced and joined the President, Magnusson and Oscar at the instrument table.

151

As Magnusson busied himself with the instruments and the television set, the President asked Henderson, "What's it like working under ice? Is it uncomfortable? Do you feel trapped with all that mass of ice over you?"

"Not a bit, sir," Henderson replied. "It's the most interesting work I've ever done. I'm not really a diver by profession, but like the rest of the gang I took special training, not only in diving but on pipelines and all the new fangled equipment we've got here."

"You mean you didn't do any diving before you started this job?"

"Yes, sir, that's correct," replied Henderson.

"And how long have you been at it now?"

"Just a little over six months. That's how long it's taken us to get these two pipeline systems organized and put together in position. When you first start at this business it's difficult to get used to the weightlessness condition under which we have to work, but once you get used to it, there's no problem. One of the things that really helps us is the sub-igloo. I don't really know how to describe it except that it's a big plastic ball into which a diver can go to rest at fifty or a hundred or two hundred feet down and get a new supply of oxygen rather than having to come up all the way to the surface. It's an invention of Dr. Joe MacInnis. He's one of the world's leading underwater scientists — a Canadian."

"What about underwater wildlife around here?" the President said. "I'd guess there really isn't anything."

"That isn't the case at all, Mr. President. I've seen all kinds of seals, walrus and whales, particularly the beluga whale and the narwhal — that's a small whale with a great spear on its nose. The water is as clear as a bell, and with the strong sunlight even through the ice you can see for a long distance. It's really something to be working just a

152

few feet under water and see these great beasts swimming by. As a matter of fact, this whole area is just teeming with wildlife. It's incredible."

Magnusson interrupted. "Pressurization has started!"

Pressurization began at 6:10 exactly, with the flow of gas following a 50-gallon oil plug through each of the pipes. All of them had immediately resumed their normal circular shape.

By 6:20 the instruments indicated that gas now filled each of the pipes 50 per cent of the way across, by 6:25 three-quarters of the way.

On the left-hand television screen the tower line sat stable.

On the right-hand screen the pipeline of the concrete system started to move. Slowly at first, then more and more rapidly it twisted and tugged at the cable locking it to the channel floor.

The four men watched the screen in fascination. Magnusson muttered, "Christ, I hope the cable holds."

At that very instant the winch lock on the ballast block was ripped apart by a mighty upward pull. Unleashed, the pipe gathered speed and instantly disappeared from the view of the television camera. Magnusson's computer-like mind told him that the loosened pipe would surface at almost 150 miles an hour, and would take only six or seven seconds before it smashed against the bottom of the ice with incredible force.

He shouted at the President, "Let's get out of here fast!" All four men made a rush for the entrance of the dome. In a near-panic they broke from it into the crisp sun-filled cold of the Arctic morning. The ice beneath their feet shook, vibrated and lifted. Four hundred yards to the south the frozen white surface under the long line of red plastic domes exploded upwards, lifting and showering cascades of shattered ice high into the air, spinning domes off in every direction. The noise was like a massive clap of rolling, unceasing thunder, deafening and continuing as the huge pipeline, moving with the force and speed of a projectile, burst through the ice, still whipping and thrashing about like a reptile gone mad.

As the thick ice rose in front of them, the President stood transfixed by the fantastic sight.

As the ice rose to its peak and the pipeline broke past it into the air, fissures began to race outward from the point of impact.

The President could see the crack coming, but it was moving so rapidly he had no time to move. In an instant it was by him. The ice almost under his right foot opened to a fissure about a yard wide. As he turned, startled, to look into the frigid water which had suddenly appeared, his right foot slipped. Thrashing wildly to regain his balance the President of the United States of America fell toward the crevasse.

Magnusson, standing just to his left, using all his power — and using it roughly — caught the President's parka. With a mighty heave he pulled the President back from the edge just as he was going to fall into the water.

As the President hit the ice flat on his back, the crevasse slammed closed as quickly as it had opened.

The writhing pipeline had broken clear of the ice and rose about a hundred feet in the air, where it hung momentarily. The thundering noise of the cascade of ice falling back to the surface was joined by a piercing, whistling sound like a balloon deflating, as the holes in the pipe ripped by the ice allowed the natural gas to escape. The enormous pressure in the pipes was gradually relieved. The rampaging snake slowly fell back onto the water and its fractured cover of ice fragments, then disappeared through it. As the pipe, still hissing and losing pressure, sank beneath the surface, the massive upheaval totally subsided.

Magnusson helped the President to his feet. His face was white. "Are you O.K.? I didn't think I'd be able to grab you."

The President took a deep breath. "God Almighty, what a sight! Son, I haven't been so close since the war. You saved my life for sure. You shook me up some, but I'm all right now. Let's go and have a look."

The four men ran quickly back into the dome. On the television monitor the tower pipe was still where it had been. Magnusson hurriedly scanned the gauges. "Sir, it's looking good. The towers are rock-solid on the bottom and the pipe is up to full pressure. We've got a pipeline!"

The President shook his hand and placed his arm on Magnusson's shoulder. "Harold, you and your team have really done a job up here. A whole lot of people are going to know about it before I'm through."

The hush in the House of Commons was complete. The Prime Minister was speaking.

"This may well be the single most urgent and direct crisis, apart from war, which Canada has ever had to face. The United States has not only given us a three-pronged ultimatum, but has specified that the answer to that ultimatum must be given by six o'clock this evening. I have asked the President to extend that time, but he has flatly refused. Therefore, the Commons and the Senate must deal with the ultimatum within the time left to us.

"At twelve noon emergency sessions of the House and Senate will begin. At that time, appropriate resolutions will be placed before both bodies. The form of the resolution has already been made known to all of you.

"From the very beginning, I have thought it absolutely essential that an opportunity be given to every member of Parliament to be informed as thoroughly as possible on the general background of this crisis. I have therefore asked the ministries most directly concerned to prepare a presentation. In this way, you will be informed of the events which have led up to the current situation, Canada's relationship with the United States and the status of the government's dealings with the native people of the Northwest Territories and the Yukon. You will also receive reports on the Mackenzie Valley pipeline, the Arctic Islands gas reserves, the question of ownership of the natural gas resources, and the transportation systems being considered with a view to getting the gas out.

"Each minister has been asked to limit his presentation to twenty-five minutes. Fifteen minutes will be devoted to a point-by-point briefing. Ten minutes will be set aside for questions and answers. Questions are to be submitted in writing and given to the pages, who will deliver them to the Speaker.

"We have a lot of ground to cover. This is no time to be attaching blame to any ministry of the past or of the present. Further to this end, I have instructed the ministers and their staffs that in the presentations to be made to you this morning I do not want any opinions given; I just want the facts.

"All parties have proposed that I chair this session. I have agreed to do so, and I have made it clear that I will insist on the time limits being strictly adhered to, both in the presentations and in the question-and-answer periods.

"I would be obliged if the Minister for External Affairs would lead off."

As Porter sat down he suddenly became conscious of the deep, attentive silence filling the Commons Chamber. This was the moment at which the burden of carrying the full responsibility shifted from his shoulders alone, to be shared by the men and women who crowded that vast hall. They sensed this, they knew it, they accepted the responsibility. And with that responsibility came apprehension and the stimulation of knowing that they themselves were participating in this most difficult of all Canadian crises.

The Minister for External Affairs was on his feet at the lectern.

"Prime Minister," Robert Gendron began, "Honourable Members, Honourable Members of the Senate, Honourable Premiers, ladies and gentlemen...."

157

After reviewing the history of the Arctic resource development, the Minister continued, "Negotiations with the Americans for the acquisition and transportation of natural gas have been going on for years. At the beginning of the seventies we held a series of discussions with them regarding a trans-Canada route for movement of the Prudhoe Bay and Mackenzie Delta gas into the Midwestern States. This resulted in the Mackenzie Valley pipeline which is now undergoing tests.

"But in other areas we have failed to come to an agreement. As far back as the days of Mr. Walter Hickel, the Secretary of the Interior, and his successor, Mr. Rogers Morton, the concept of a continental energy policy between the United States and Canada began to take shape. The Americans clearly wanted to have full access to all Canadian fossil fuels just as if Canada were part of the United States. The effect would be that Canada would share its fuel resources with the United States and take on the U.S. energy shortages in return.

"The Americans have doggedly pursued their attempts to negotiate such a continental energy policy with us. Just as doggedly, Canada has refused, with the result that no agreement exists for the transfer of the natural gas which lies in the Canadian Arctic archipelago.

"If the Americans had been prepared to negotiate with us for the natural gas alone, without attempting to wrap the whole thing up in one continental policy, it is very likely that they would have been given access to one-third of the reserves now proven in the Arctic Islands, and the transportation system would have been in preparation.

"I turn now to consideration of the American attitude toward Canada so that you may conclude what the Americans would be prepared to do to enforce the ultimatum. But first, a few remarks about the American presence in the world scene.

"During the 1950's, the United States, under President Eisenhower and the Secretary of State, John Foster Dulles, accepted the so-called domino theory of communist expansion. Dulles reasoned that if one country in Southeast Asia was to fall to the communists, then the country next to it would fall, and so on until all the nations had fallen into communist hands. This he conceived to be a direct threat to the United States and to the freedom of the world. On the basis of this theory, the United States had a right, indeed even a responsibility, to intervene militarily wherever a communist takeover seemed possible. Thus when the French were driven out of Vietnam in 1954, the United States refused to sign the Geneva armistice, the only western nation to do so. Ultimately the Americans moved to thwart the general election which was planned in that country. It did so on the ground that it was clear that Hanoi forces would win. As a result, the Americans became involved in a direct military intervention on an enormous scale which lasted for a period of nineteen years.

"The point I want to make is that in the case of Vietnam, and before that in Korea and elsewhere in the world, the United States has never hesitated to use, or to threaten to use, military force if it felt that its own national interests or security were threatened.

"The U.S. continues to maintain strategic bases in various parts of the world — air bases, radar sites, submarines and surface vessels, together with a vast armory of sophisticated missiles.

"Granted, then, that the United States has the power and is prepared to use it, what support would Canada have in its struggle with that giant? Very little. Under President Nixon, many of the tensions between the United States and the Soviet Union, on the one hand, and the United States and China on the other, were substantially eased, with the result that the relationship of the United

States to both these countries is on a stable level. Therefore, it would be impossible to expect that in this crisis Canada could depend on any diplomatic or other support from the Soviet Union, and certainly not from China.

"Probably the best we could expect would be the support of world opinion against the action taken by the President. Frankly, I do not expect world criticism to have any effect whatsoever on the President. Canada stands alone, without any hope of defending itself militarily.

"On the other hand, I do not think the President would be prepared to take Canada by force, thereby risking the confidence of all the major powers and indeed of the world. The spectacle of the United States seizing an ally, its major trading partner, is one which I cannot visualize. Furthermore, there is little doubt in my mind that the President can achieve most of his objectives by hard bargaining now that he has stressed that the United States needs the fossil fuels immediately and that he is not prepared to accept any further delays.

"Let us for the moment assume that the United States will act against Canada by way of sanctions should we fail to accede to the ultimatum. There is no doubt that this is in the President's mind. As we all know, he imposed an embargo yesterday at noon against the flow of investment capital into Canada, though he later withdrew that sanction when we countered with the threat to cut off all exports of oil and gas.

"Sanctions have undoubtedly been the United States' prime weapon against its trading partners who have gained an economic advantage. The States first employed such measures in earnest a decade ago when, as a result of a deficit in world trade, it began to take steps to protect its dollar and to support its work force. As foreign goods became competitive in quality as well as price, and as the outflow of American dollars around the world continued to exceed inflow of capital, it became apparent that the American dollar could not withstand world competition. It began to fall in value, a reflection of the fall in relative productivity of the United States' industrial complex.

"Finally, in 1971, as a reaction to the thrust of foreign products into the American market, President Nixon imposed a 10 per cent surcharge on all imports of manufactured goods. It is significant that he very carefully excluded from this category the natural resources necessary to keep the U.S. industrial machine in operation. Canada was caught in that net, despite the fact that we were the major trading partner of the United States. After some revaluations of foreign currencies, President Nixon withdrew the impost. Nevertheless, shortly after, the United States government created the Domestic Incentive Sales Corporation program. DISC was designed to attract American manufacturing capital back to the United States, to induce American corporations which had manufacturing subsidiaries in foreign countries such as Canada to shut those subsidiaries down and return the jobs to the U.S. The device was, and still is, a very simple one, and while the DISC program cannot be classified technically as a sanction, it nevertheless demonstrates the type of America-first action which that country is prepared to take, regardless of its trading partners or neighbouring countries.

"In 1975, the United States enacted the Burke-Hartke Act, which provides even more protection by making it possible to put a ceiling on the import of any given commodity into the United States. As you well know, this has worked a serious hardship on Canadian industries, the majority of which are subsidiaries of United States firms, and has created an enormous impediment to the sale of

Canadian-manufactured goods in the United States, Canada's biggest market.

"Thus there is little doubt in my mind that the United States will not hesitate to impose economic sanctions to achieve the aims of the ultimatum.

"That concludes my brief, Prime Minister. Now if I may, I will deal with the questions in the order in which they have been delivered."

Gendron stopped and turned to speak to his deputy, Max Peterson, sitting on his right. Peterson had been collecting and making notes on the question papers. He gathered them together and handed them all to the Minister.

Gendron put the stack of papers on the lectern and said, "Ladies and gentlemen, I have about nine minutes left of my time allocation. I'll try to get through as many of these questions as I can.

"The first question is, 'Is there any evidence of troop movement in Detroit or Buffalo, or in any of the northern American cities?'

"The answer is, 'No, there is not, although as of yesterday morning at nine o'clock there was a sharp increase in the number of bomber and fighter flights over Canadian territory by the USAF. We regard these overflights as merely a form of intimidation rather than any preparation for military action.'

"The next question is, 'If the flow of United States investment capital to Canada is cut off, what are the chances of getting an increased volume from Western Europe, and especially from the Middle East members of the Organization of Petroleum Exporting Countries?'

"That is an excellent question. As you know, the members of OPEC — which includes Saudi Arabia, Iran, Iraq, Kuwait, Venezuela, Libya, Algeria, and others — are tremendously wealthy as a result of their sale of oil to the

162

United States. They export 80 per cent of the petroleum on the international market and control 70 per cent of the world's oil reserves. They are therefore very powerful.

"It is regrettable, perhaps, that Canada does not belong to OPEC. We were invited to join two years ago, but when pressure was put on by the United States to decline, we did so. Nevertheless, I have instructed our ambassadors at Beirut and Teheran to set up emergency meetings today with the heads of government of all the OPEC countries in the Middle East. Our Ambassador in Italy is in Libya and will also go on to Algeria. The Ambassador will explain the nature of the emergency and seek immediate investment support in the event that sanctions are imposed.

"At this point we don't know what the response of the government leaders of the OPEC countries will be. I believe there is an enormous base of sympathy on their part for Canada. They realize that our relationship with the United States has slowly become more difficult over the years. I can assure you if the OPEC countries do support Canada with investment funds, it will be on the condition that we join their organization. One of OPEC's reasons for existence is that, since its members control so much of the world's supply of oil, they can apply pressure on the United States, which now must buy over 60 per cent of its oil and energy supply from foreign sources.

"There is one further point. . . . Excuse me for just a moment." The Minister for External Affairs hesitated, then left the lectern and walked around the end of the table to his right to where the Prime Minister sat. The two whispered together briefly, and then Gendron returned to the lectern.

"I thought I should check with the Prime Minister on what I am going to tell you next. As you know, the Prime Minister secured the lifting of the American investment embargo by threatening to cut off exports of oil and gas to the United States. He had hoped that the threat would be strong enough to cause the President to lift the ultimatum altogether, but it was not. What the Prime Minister has now agreed that I may reveal to you is that our ambassadors have been instructed to say that if Canada is forced to apply such a counter-sanction, we will join OPEC provided the OPEC countries agree to institute a similar embargo and cut off all supplies of oil to the United States."

At that, the silence of the audience was broken. There were gasps, and people turned to each other, first with looks of astonishment and then with smiles of approval as the full implications of this move became evident.

When the buzz of conversation had diminished, Gendron went on.

"Unfortunately I have no idea whether we can have an answer from all these countries within the time limit given to us. We have sent a message to every head of state in OPEC outlining our position and asking for support, but it will be the attendance of the appropriate Canadian ambassador that will be important in securing a commitment. With good luck, we may have some answers by the time the vote is taken at five o'clock this evening."

Gendron's assistant, to his left, plucked at his sleeve, and pointed to his watch. Gendron concluded, "Prime Minister, ladies and gentlemen, I have used up my time allocation. I now turn you over to the Honourable Otto Gunther, Minister of Energy, Mines and Resources, and his Deputy Minister, Claude Lafrance."

The Twin Otter was circling over Placer Lake thirty-five miles southwest of Aklavik. This was the spot marked Number Two on Sam's map, the site of the bomb that was due to explode first in sequence.

They had worked late the night before, after Sam's departure on the government Hercules, going over the map and rechecking carefully the locations and the planned explosion times. Bessie peered intently as the plane passed over the point where the pipeline crossed the stream feeding the lake. "This is it," she said.

Ray turned and shouted to the pilot, "O.K., Sandy, you can put her down on the lake."

They still had lots of time. If they could find this bomb and get it safely defused without unexpected problems, they'd likely get to the rest of the bombs all right.

The pilot completed his turn and headed northeast to touch down on the lake about half a mile from the pipe crossing. He landed in the soft snow and taxied back to get as close to the pipeline as he could. Then he shut down the engines.

Bessie and the Staff Sergeant collected their gear — snowshoes, a shovel and a small tool kit containing a set of screwdrivers, a pair of pliers and insulating tape. Then Ray opened the rear passenger door, sat down on the aircraft floor with his feet outboard and put on his snowshoes before jumping onto the snow-covered surface of the lake. Bessie followed.

Pulling their parka hoods up over their heads, they set off at a fast pace with the Staff Sergeant leading. They crossed the shore of the lake, passed through a heavy stand of jackpine, and broke into the pipeline clearing a few feet away from where the pipe crossed the stream and Sam had planted the explosive charge. When they entered the clearing, Bessie moved ahead of the Staff Sergeant, taking the small shovel from his hand as she passed him. She led the way to the pipe and located the spot where she thought the bomb was buried. Even though Sam and she had been there only two days earlier, the windblown snow had obliterated any tracks they had left, and all evidence of their tampering was gone. Gently she began to scrape away the top layer of snow with a sideways motion of the shovel, but then she stopped and handed it back to the Staff Sergeant saying, "Maybe I shouldn't use the shovel. If I hit the timing mechanism I might set it off."

She began to scoop the snow away with her fur-mittened hands, slowly and cautiously. Finally she touched something hard. She said, "I've got it."

The Staff Sergeant said, "O.K., Bessie, I'll handle it now."

He took Bessie's place. He could see the corner of the blue plastic bag at the bottom of the hole, about a foot down, and he scraped away some more snow until he could see clearly the entire top of the package. Using both hands, he pulled it up towards him. It came easily, for the snow had not been packed down. Moving very carefully, he backed away from the pipe for a distance of about ten feet, and laid the package gently in the snow. Because of its weight, it sank several inches into the surface. It was going to be difficult to work on.

Ray said, "Bessie, if you'd come around facing me and bring the front of one of your snowshoes in between mine,

166

the three together should give me a flat surface I can work on."

Gingerly Ray lifted the package out of the snow and laid it on the snowshoes. He pulled off his fur mitts and undid the twist fastener around the neck of the bag. With his left hand he held the bottom of the bag and attempted to reach inside to grasp the timer and detonator. "It won't work. I'll have to cut the bag open. I don't want to pull on the wires to get the explosives out."

He took out a short, extremely sharp knife and slit the plastic bag from end to end, revealing the entire explosive apparatus. Quickly he checked the timer. Correct, as listed. It had been set to go off forty-three hours from the time the bomb was laid. Just an hour to go. Then he examined the detonator carefully. The arming device was in and set, the all-important defusing wheel had its white marker in the correct position. Cautiously Ray placed the index finger and thumb of his left hand on the edge of the arming device to steady it, then slowly he rotated the wheel clockwise until the marker disappeared and it came to a full stop.

It was twenty degrees below zero, but the Staff Sergeant was soaking wet with perspiration. While, as he had said, he knew something about explosives, he was far from being an expert, and here he was, deep in the bush, relying totally on a quick briefing given to him by Sam Allen. If that briefing had been wrong ... !

Now that the timer had been disarmed, Ray picked up the pair of pliers and quickly cut the connection between the plastic explosives and the arming device. He got stiffly up from his crouched position, looked down at Bessie from his great height and said quietly, "Bessie, I can understand that you people feel strongly about what the white man is doing to you, but to play around with this stuff you

167

and Sam must be right out of your goddam minds." Then he bent over and picked up the explosive, stuffed it in his left pocket and took the small tool kit, arming device and timer. Bessie didn't reply, but her eyes showed the strain. She picked up the shovel and fell quietly in behind Ray as he headed back toward the aircraft. As they emerged from the jackpines at the edge of the lake, Sandy started up the engines. As they climbed on board, he said, "Everything O.K.?"

Ray nodded. "Everything's O.K., but this is the best way I know of to get a heart attack. Let's hit Number One next. That's up to the northwest. We'll do it, and then come straight back south, doing the rest of them in the series. We've got the tough one out of the way now."

The pilot nodded, did his pre-takeoff check, and shoved the throttle forward. The aircraft skied a few feet down the track and was almost immediately airborne. In five minutes they reached Number One point.

As the Minister for External Affairs was returning to his seat next to the Prime Minister, he passed Otto Gunther and his deputy on their way to the front of the Chamber. There was a general rustle in the audience as people shuffled papers and shifted positions, but by the time the Minister of Energy, Mines and Resources was established behind the lectern with his notes before him, the room was silent once again.

Gunther's bald head reflected the lights of the Chamber and the television spotlights. Already a few tiny beads of perspiration were appearing. He was not a good speaker, and it was a strain for him to address this kind of audience, or any kind of audience, for that matter. With a final nervous clearing of his throat, he began, his flat, Newfoundland accent more pronounced than usual. "Prime Minister, ladies and gentlemen ... I mean Prime Minister, Members of the Senate, Members of the House, Premiers, ladies and gentlemen: From the viewpoint of my department — I am sorry — my ministry, Energy, Mines and Resources — if I may I will refer to it as EMR — we have been ... rather, we are responsible ... that is to say, I am the minister to whom the National Energy Board reports, so we have a major interest in the amount of gas and oil which is surplus to Canada, whether it should ... whether it is sufficient to sell it to the United States. We are also interested in the financing and construction of the pipe-

lines and other kinds of transportation methods used to
get the gas out. So, for that matter, of course, are Northern
Affairs and the Ministry of the Environment and the Ministry of Transport. We don't always see eye to eye, but we
try." He coughed and wiped his head. "Also there are some
questions between us in the various ministries as to who
is responsible for what.

"I want to deal first with the Arctic Islands. I brought
some slides along to show you the places I want to talk
about." He turned and said to Lafrance, "Claude, will you
put the slides on for me? And you'd better run the machine
also, if you don't mind."

Lafrance went around the table and dropped a tray of
slides into the projector. He switched on the machine and
flicked to the first picture, a map of the Arctic Islands from
Banks across to Ellesmere, and from the Boothia Peninsula and Northwest Passage to the North Pole. Gunther
proceeded.

"On this map you can see Melville Island at the bottom
left-hand corner. The area between Melville Island on the
southwest and the Eureka area of Ellesmere Island to the
northeast is known as the Sverdrup Basin, and these
islands are called the Sverdrup Islands. Starting in 1970,
with the first strike at Drake Point on Melville Island, successful exploration work has been going on here. There are
now fifty drilling rigs on the islands, and gas finds have
been made on Melville, King Christian, Thor, Ellef Ringnes, Axel Heiberg and Ellesmere. There have also been
four oil finds, one on Banks Island to the southwest of
Melville, another on Thor, and a third on Ellesmere and
a major new discovery on Melville.

"Our best estimate on the gas reserves in the Islands is
now approximately 60-trillion cubic feet, which is about
three times the amount necessary to justify the cost of

170

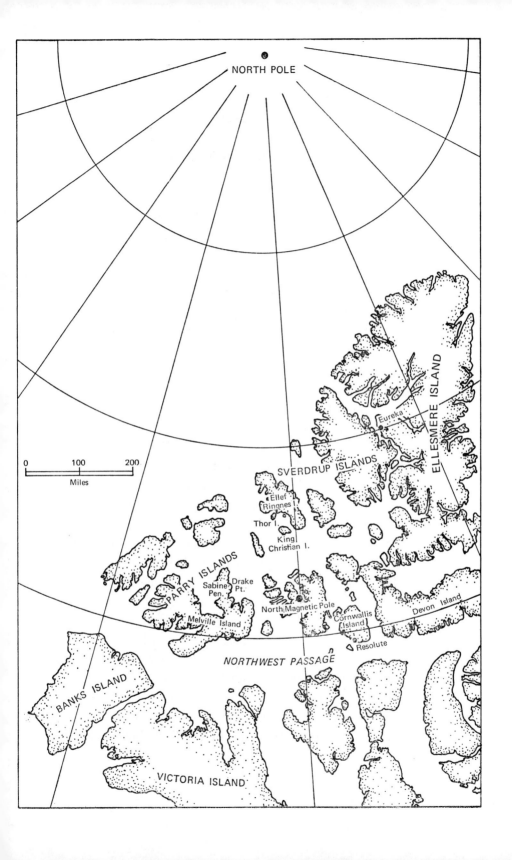

NORTH POLE

ELLESMERE ISLAND

Eureka

SVERDRUP ISLANDS

Ellef
Ringnes I.

Thor I.

King
Christian I.

PARRY ISLANDS

Drake
Pt.

Sabine
Pen.

North Magnetic Pole

Cornwallis
Island

Devon Island

Melville Island

Resolute

NORTHWEST PASSAGE

BANKS ISLAND

VICTORIA ISLAND

0   100   200
Miles

construction of a transportation system to deliver 1½-trillion cubic feet a year to the market in the United States. On the basis of a thirty-year projection, Canada needs 35-trillion cubic feet to meet its future requirements. This leaves a surplus of 25-trillion cubic feet which could be exported."

Gunther paused a moment, took out his handkerchief again and wiped his face and bald head. He was now perspiring profusely, but he struggled on, reading from his notes.

"Most of the gas reserves are held by Panarctic, which is a Canadian-controlled company, as I am sure you are all aware. It was formed in 1968 because the Canadian government was afraid that exploration wouldn't go forward in the Arctic without some incentives. It is 45 per cent owned by the government of Canada, 10 per cent by Canadian corporations such as Canadian Pacific Investment, and 45 per cent by foreign corporations. At no time have any shares of Panarctic been made available for purchase by the Canadian public — unfortunately.

"When Panarctic started to hit in 1970 with its first discovery well at Drake Point on Melville, and a later find on King Christian Island, American interests quickly appeared on the scene. Gas distribution firms in the U.S. quickly saw there was going to be a major supply on the Arctic Islands and they wanted to be there for a piece of the action. It was clear there was going to be an enormous shortage of natural gas, and they were anxious to advance exploration money to Panarctic in return for the right to purchase the gas when it was discovered. And that's what they've done. Tenneco of Houston, Columbia Natural Gas and other gas distributors have advanced Panarctic interest-free money repayable only in the event that gas is produced. Within three years of the first discoveries, the

Panarctic shareholders had put up $101-million, while the American group had invested over $75-million. Since that time, the capital input by Panarctic has remained at $101-million, but now the American investment is over $500-million.

"It can be said that because Tenneco and its associates have the first right to negotiate for the gas discovered by Panarctic, and because they have put up the lion's share of the capital . . . it can be said the American firms in effect own the gas in the ground. They own it, but they have to get permission to take it out and transport it to market.

"Now I'd like to return to the question of a continental energy policy, touched on by the Minister of External Affairs. During the Nixon administration, the Americans decided that an over-all policy concerned with all available forms of energy was essential throughout North America. They pointed out that since the United States and Canada occupy the same continent, and since the United States had in effect paid for the discoveries made in the Canadian Archipelago, it made sense to have an agreement regarding the distribution of the products resulting from those discoveries.

"For the Americans, a continental energy policy meant that Canada would share all of its energy resources with the United States, which in turn meant that we would have to share the shortages as well. When the President says that Canada has refused to agree to make available to the United States the Arctic Islands gas, he is not correct. What we have refused to do is enter into a continental energy policy agreement, of which gas would only be a part. I am of the firm view that if negotiations had proceeded on the basis of gas alone, the Americans could have had a commitment for the Arctic reserves long ago, and the transportation system would have been well on its way by now.

173

"In a way, Canada has been fortunate that an agreement wasn't reached. Up until the middle of the last decade, we were practically giving our gas and oil away. To obtain exploration rights in the Mackenzie Delta and the Arctic Islands, a company was only required to put down a deposit of between 5 cents and 25 cents per acre. Then, if drilling was successful, it would pay a royalty of 5 per cent on all production for the first five years (if the find was north of latitude 70 degrees) and 10 per cent thereafter, or (if the find was below latitude 70 degrees) 5 per cent for the first three years and 10 per cent thereafter. Anyone can see that this works out at not much more than bank interest on the capital which had been given away in the ground. Thus Canada stood to gain practically nothing from the sale of oil and gas.

"Compare that kind of giveaway with what the Middle East countries have done and are now doing in terms of retaining ownership of the fossil fuels in the ground and taxing the product. With royalties, taxes and payment money, they get a return of between five and six dollars a barrel for oil which costs twenty cents to produce. It's little wonder that the Middle East and Mediterranean members of OPEC have become among the richest nations in the world with very little effort. In fact, the control of billions upon billions of American dollars, in the hands of the leaders of these countries, has enabled them to manipulate the American dollar in world markets and cause serious changes in the value of the dollar from time to time.

"Fortunately Canada has smartened up a bit in its dealings. We have issued new leases covering the drilled acreage in the North. Under the new terms, a fair share of the proceeds of the sale at well-head will go to the Canadian people, in export taxes and a royalty of 25 per cent on all production in the Islands and the Delta. The U.S. oil

174

and gas companies have been extremely annoyed at the new terms, but for Canadians they could provide a return of 50 per cent of the market price of the gas, and in effect a yearly income equivalent to all federal expenditures. Thus it is certainly in Canada's interests to arrange for the export of these resources, provided Canada's future needs are protected.

"Now I see my time has just about run out. Perhaps I can answer one question."

Gunther took one of the notes which had been left beside the lectern on the table. "Why shouldn't Canada enter into a continental energy agreement with the United States?"

"Well, I can't answer for the previous administrations, and I may not be able to answer for this one. . . ." He glanced down toward the Prime Minister.

Robert Porter stood up. "If I may, I'll answer that question for Mr. Gunther. It is a most difficult one. I don't want him to bear a responsibility which he should not have.

"It boils down quite simply to a question of sovereignty. If Canada is to remain an independent nation with its own goals and objectives and a political and judicial system quite different from that of the United States, then it is clear that we must be as free as possible to plan our own economic development and in particular the use to which our natural resources, especially those which are non-renewable, are put. It is apparent to all of us that we already live in the economic and cultural shadow of the United States. As a result, it is most difficult at times to maintain a position of independence.

"If we should agree to a continental policy on all sources of energy, it is clear that we would then have to share the United States' shortages. The Americans are dependent now on foreign imports for 60 per cent of their energy. Canada is self-sufficient. If the two countries were to

175

merge their interests in energy, Canada would join the United States in being largely dependent on offshore suppliers. This would undoubtedly make us even more vulnerable to economic domination from abroad, and we would find it almost impossible to maintain our independence. For these reasons, Canada has taken its present position, and I can see no reason for changing at this moment, although I must confess that with the ultimatum now handed to us by the President, it is very likely that we can expect other pressure to be applied.

"Clearly, what is at issue is not so much the access to the energy reserves of the Canadian Arctic as the whole question of an independent future for Canadians."

Air Force One / (Resolute Bay)
7:57 a.m., CDT

The President settled down in his favourite spot, the captain's seat in the Boeing 747, Air Force One. He had just taken off from Resolute Bay for Washington.

Things were moving on schedule. This early morning start should get him back into the White House before three o'clock in the afternoon. It was not to be a direct trip, however. He had one more visit in mind.

They were climbing sharply, headed south over the Northwest Passage. Suddenly the President pulled back the power and levelled off at 2,000 feet. And then, smiling to himself at the startled glance Colonel Mike Wypich threw his way, he turned the big bird in a slow arc to proceed east down the Passage.

Answering the captain's unspoken question he said, "Don't panic, Mike. We're going to inspect the newest, toughest ice-breaker in the world. You don't know it, the Canadians don't know it — yet — but the *Polar Star* is in the Northwest Passage, and she should steam by Resolute Bay in about an hour and a half! This is her first shakedown voyage, and we're going to drop by."

Wypich asked, "How did she get up here so fast, Mr. President?"

"Very simple, Mike. She was in Baffin Bay last week, pretty close to Lancaster Sound, the eastern entrance of the Northwest Passage. I thought it might be useful to show the flag this morning, so I instructed the captain to take her past Resolute Bay as close to shore as he could safely go, and then head east toward McClure Strait. That's where the *Manhattan* got stuck in 1972. I'd like the captain to go right through McClure Strait. The underwater ice formations they call pingoes may make it difficult, but the *Polar Star* has two pretty sophisticated sets of sonar sounding gear which should make it possible for her to get through all right. The United States claims that the Northwest Passage is high seas, Mike, and I want to show Canada we mean what we say."

"There she is, sir," Mike exclaimed. "Twelve o'clock and about five miles coming straight at us."

"Beautiful!" said the President. "Beautiful! Let's have a good look."

As Air Force One approached the *Polar Star* from the west, the President let down to 1,000 feet and turned slightly to the south so he could pass by the ship and have a good view of her.

"Beautiful" he said once again. "Mike, see if you can crank up the captain on the blower. His name is Anderson. You can probably get him on the emergency frequency."

Within forty-five seconds Mike had the captain on the radio. The President said, "Captain Anderson, this is the President. I want to congratulate you on a first-class job in getting that beautiful big ship into the Northwest Passage and over here as quickly as you have. Try to get in as close to Resolute Bay as you can when you go by. I don't want anybody to miss the fact you're here carrying the flag. I know you should probably keep twelve miles offshore to stay clear of Canadian waters, but I think you ought to bend it a little this morning. Do you think you can get the *Polar Star* through McClure Strait?"

Anderson came back, "Yes, sir, no question about it. The pingoes have been charted and I have a channel through them, so that shouldn't be any problem. And with my 75,000 horsepower, I'm sure I can get through that ice whether it's ten feet or fourteen feet thick."

"Fine," the President said. "Mighty fine. Now remember, Captain, it's important to the United States that the *Polar Star* get through McClure Strait. It's also important that she doesn't sink, of course."

"Yes, sir."

"I'll be keeping an eye on you once you get into the McClure, Captain. Good luck."

"Thank you, sir," said Anderson.

The President did one more circle around his prize polar ice-breaker — 14,000 tons of super-hard, ice-fortified steel.

As the President watched, the gray-painted hull of the *Polar Star* sliced neatly through a three-foot pan of ice as if it wasn't there. The President guessed she was steaming about 20 knots. He could see the two helicopters which she carried on board to the rear of the great funnel. The high bridge, located just slightly ahead of midships, was strewn with electronic gear and wires. Otherwise the great ship was completely uncluttered. Despite her vast bulk and weight, the *Polar Star* was as trim and sleek as a racer. She had an appearance of grace, lightness, and speed which belied her function as a floating battering-ram.

As he finished his last circling turn over the bow, the President said, "She's the best in the world, Mike. For the United States, that's the way it should be."

With that, he put Air Force One on its course for Washington, and poured climbing power into the engines. "You have control, Mike. Head her for the barn; I've got work to do."

179

Ottawa / 8:59 a.m., EDT

The Minister of Indian Affairs and Northern Development, Pierre Allard from Northern Manitoba, a tall, thin man with a long, sharp-featured face and grey-streaked straight hair, strode briskly to the lectern. On his way, he set his tray of slides on the projector and switched immediately to a map of Canada on which had been outlined the Mackenzie Valley Corridor.

Obviously not a man to waste time, he began as soon as he reached the microphone. "Like the minister who preceded me, I have not held this portfolio very long — only about seven weeks — but I feel confident that the background knowledge I acquired before taking office, added to what I have learned since, will enable me to make clear the situation as it exists in the Mackenzie Valley Corridor, particularly as it relates to the rights of the native people.

"The Mackenzie River, as you can see from the map, flows north from Great Slave Lake to the Mackenzie Delta, where it spreads and enters the Arctic Ocean. The wide river valley, called the Corridor, is a relatively habitable area as opposed to the barren Arctic tundra. That is because the river itself softens the climate, permitting trees to grow and providing food and shelter for men and animals. For centuries, Indians have lived in the treed area and Eskimos in the tundra at the north end of the river and to the east toward Hudson Bay. In ancient times, the Indian and Eskimo were mortal enemies. There were many

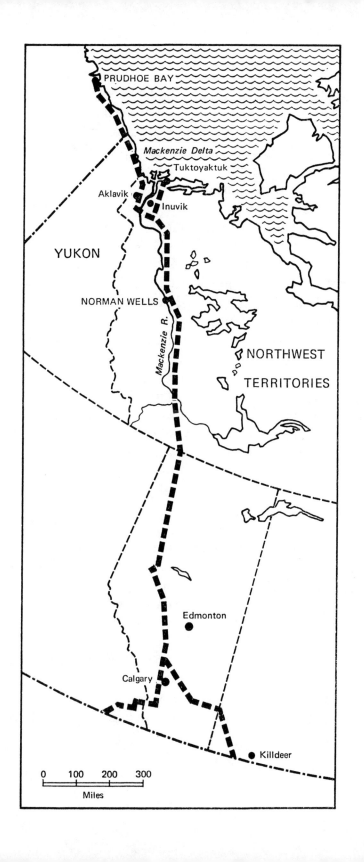

PRUDHOE BAY

Mackenzie Delta
Tuktoyaktuk

Aklavik
Inuvik

YUKON

NORMAN WELLS

Mackenzie R.

NORTHWEST

TERRITORIES

Edmonton

Calgary

Killdeer

0   100   200   300

Miles

bloody battles waged between the two races.

"The Mackenzie River has been the prime route into the Western Arctic since its discovery by Alexander Mackenzie in 1789. In the early days, canoes carried trading goods and furs along its waters. In modern times, barges transport products north to Norman Wells and Tuktoyaktuk. Recently the aircraft has begun to play a major role in the Corridor as well as throughout the entire Arctic. During the 1960's and into the 70's, Pacific Western, a regional air carrier was securely established, running from Edmonton to Yellowknife and Inuvik. And Inuvik, a relatively new town situated to the east of Aklavik in the Mackenzie Delta, is now the regional centre for that entire area.

"After 1968, when the Prudhoe Bay discovery was announced, the pace of exploration in the Mackenzie Delta region quickened. Then, with the first discovery of oil at Atkinson Point on the Tuktoyaktuk Peninsula in January 1970, the importance of the area as a source of hydrocarbons, both gas and oil, was firmly established, and drilling rigs really began to get to work. By the winter of 1972, there were thirteen rigs in operation in the Delta. Major finds had been made on Richards Island as well as on the Tuktoyaktuk Peninsula, and natural gas was being found in increasing amounts. By 1974 there were sufficient reserves to meet the minimum requirements for the creation of a pipeline from the Mackenzie Delta to the American market even without the Prudhoe Bay flow.

"Air transport moved regularly and by charter down the Corridor from Edmonton and Yellowknife into the Delta. Barge traffic increased to such an extent that by 1974 the Northern Transportation Company, a CNR subsidiary, was carrying 500,000 tons of goods annually. So even then the Corridor was very much alive.

"In 1972 a decision was made to build a highway from

182

Yellowknife to Inuvik and Tuktoyaktuk. Construction was begun, but it soon ground to a halt because of a lack of government co-ordination. The enterprise was revived and set on course again, however, after the Prime Minister had intervened, and a reasonable degree of inter-departmental liaison had been established. Eventually the highway, which paralleled the route for the gas pipeline, was completed, and has been extensively used in the pipeline construction.

"The next element of transportation to appear in the Mackenzie Valley Corridor was the pipeline itself, forty-eight inches in diameter, and laid underground or in mounds called berms.

"Now, as you are all aware, what is happening is that in the Northwest Territories and the Yukon, where the pipe is most remote from points of service and repair, explosions are now regularly taking place, destroying segments of the pipe. It is believed that the sabotage is the work of certain native groups, but since no one has been caught in the act and no one has been charged, it's impossible to say. Nevertheless, the native peoples have made no secret of the fact that they are prepared to take such action if their rights to the land in the Northwest Territories are not recognized.

"There has been no such recognition. It was not until 1973, as a result of the findings of the Supreme Court of Canada in the Nishga Indians' case, that Prime Minister Trudeau was forced to agree to negotiate. Talks did begin, but collapsed almost immediately. The result is that there is no agreement with the native people.

"The Indians, Eskimos, and Métis of the Northwest Territories and the Yukon claim that they have the rights to the land as the original inhabitants. By far the greater part of the Corridor is occupied by Indians and Eskimos

183

with whom no treaty has ever been signed. Some of the Indians in the Lower Mackenzie Valley signed treaties during the 1800's, and the native people point to these as evidence that the white man recognized their original rights.

"They have naturally been angered to see drilling rigs appear on their lands at Tuktoyaktuk, on Cape Bathurst, on Banks Island, and in the Mackenzie Delta, without their permission. They have watched while the white man destroyed their hunting grounds and the terrain and has pierced the permafrost with his rigs to drill down and secure rich deposits of gas and oil without paying them any compensation.

"And so they began, ten years ago, to gather together in groups such as the Committee for Original Peoples' Entitlement at Inuvik, the Indian Brotherhood of the Northwest Territories, the Indian Brotherhood of the Yukon, the Inuit Tapirisat, and others. They have rallied their people and have presented their claims to the white man. They said, 'Look, you are doing everything you can to help the foreign oil companies come into our lands and rip up our ground and put in drilling rigs to take out oil and gas, but you have given us no sign that you are prepared to settle as the government of the United States settled with the native people of Alaska when it came time to take the oil and gas from Prudhoe Bay and build a pipeline across to Valdez. Why are we, the native people in Canada, different from the native people in Alaska? We want not only the jobs that go with pipeline construction, but we want more than anything else to have a fair settlement for our lands and for the rich minerals that lie under them.'

"So we who live in the rest of Canada, and the government, have only ourselves to blame for the bombings. We have been too cheap and too short-sighted, at least until

184

this time, to settle fairly with our native people and to bring the American and French oil and gas owners in the Mackenzie Delta into the settlement. After all, even a poor Métis like myself can understand the frustration of the native people when they see themselves being defrauded.

"One further point is this. There has been much agitation in the North because they have not been permitted their own elected representative government. I have been instructed by the Prime Minister to advise this meeting that it is the intention of this government to place legislation before this Parliament very shortly to give self-government, in a modified provincial form, to both territories. When that occurs, the archaic system of government by the Minister or the Deputy Minister or the Assistant Deputy Minister in Ottawa will come to a long-overdue end.

"That concludes my statement, and now I will proceed to the questions."

The pages had brought only three pieces of paper to Allard as he was speaking. He glanced quickly over the top one and said, "The first question is double-barrelled. It asks which of the ministries has been responsible for negotiating with the United States on the Arctic natural gas and oil, and whether the American complaint about dealing with Ottawa is justified."

Allard paused a moment, ran a hand through his thick hair, and shifted uncomfortably from one foot to the other. "This is a very difficult question. The answer to the first part is that it has been mainly the responsibility of the Minister of Energy, Mines and Resources. However, because the natural gas and oil lie within the Northwest Territories and the Yukon, my ministry has historically felt that it, and not EMR, controlled the resources. My people feel that they should have just as much say in the matter as the EMR people do, not only in dealing with the Americans, but also in the setting of policy on royalties and the rules and regulations governing the drilling and exploration activities in the Arctic.

"Quite frankly, we've been involved in a leadership brawl over the work of the Advisory Committee on Northern Development. This committee, made up of senior civil servants from all the ministries with responsibilities in the Territories, makes recommendations to the various ministers. In the past, the committee has been so strong and the ministers so weak that virtually all the recommendations have been accepted without question. As a result, we have had policy-making, in fact, government, by a committee of civil servants.

"Each of the ministries responsible for the Territories is jealous of the others. Thus, there is little communication between them, even at the advisory committee, and there is example after example of overlapping of activity in the departments because of a failure to communicate. What has been truly lacking has been a committee at the ministerial level, with a strong leader who can cut across the decisions of all the ministries. It is also deplorable that we have not had, up until this time, a clearcut statement of national goals and objectives for the Canadian North.

"Therefore, the answer to the second part of the question, Do the Americans have a valid complaint? must be Yes, because if Canadians themselves find it difficult to deal with bureaucracy, to get decisions, then the Americans must find it a hundred times more difficult and frustrating.

"As you are all aware, the Prime Minister has already announced a major reorganization of the civil service and a radical change in the government's approach to the Northwest Territories and the Yukon. He has already declared that he will create a Ministry of State for the

Arctic under his personal leadership to which all the ministries which are now involved in the Advisory Committee will be responsible.

"Also, my ministry will soon be split, with the Indian Affairs section going to Secretary of State and the Northern Development branch to Energy, Mines and Resources. These two areas of responsibility have been conflicting. On the one hand we deal with and protect people, and on the other encourage and assist development. That situation has not made sense, and the results have been easy to see."

At this point the Prime Minister caught Allard's eye and motioned to his watch. He responded by saying, "The Prime Minister has informed me my time is up. Thank you."

Porter rose and said, "Thank you, Pierre. I have just had word that the Minister of Defence has been held up and will not be able to make his presentation, so perhaps I can substitute for him. What I'll attempt to do is give you a status report on the Canadian armed forces so that you can weigh their role and possible effectiveness in this crisis. The regular force establishment is 55,000, and we are up to full strength. This government is in the process of withdrawing the 5,000 troops that have been on NATO duty in Europe, together with the air squadrons which support them, although we are maintaining our commitment to NATO to keep them completely air mobile so that they can be relied upon as available reserves in the event of an armed confrontation in Europe.

"In Canada, under Mobile Command, we have three CF5 fighter squadrons, and approximately 3,000 combat-ready troops.

"The reserves, that is to say the Militia, the Air Reserve, and the Naval Reserve, have been increased in strength in recent years to a present level of 30,000 men, and we are

187

working up to an establishment of 40,000.

"I have instructed the Chief of the Defence Staff to put all his troops at full alert during this crisis, not because we anticipate an attack from the United States — that would be unthinkable — but to support the civil authorities in case there are anti-American demonstrations.

"This has been a very brief statement. I don't think I need cover any more points on the military side. The next report will come from the Ministry of Transport."

Ottawa / 9:56 a.m., EDT

The Minister of Transport, Leonard Watts, began by outlining the problems inherent in transporting the natural gas from the Arctic Islands by undersea pipe. He then went on, "If this is the way the United States and its buyers, such as Tenneco, choose to go, they will obviously want access to the Islands and other parts of the Northwest Territories, and they will want the authority to set the standards for environmental protection so that construction is not hampered by regulations which are too stringent. My colleague, the Minister of the Environment, will undoubtedly have a few words to say on this subject.

"The next form of transportation is the tanker. Specially-built ice-strengthened ships equipped with massive tanks designed to carry liquefied natural gas do not exist today. Such ships would have to be at least 250,000 tons dead weight, and they would have to have special tanks for ballast so that they could cut through the permanent ice on their way into the Islands.

"There's a very serious question in my mind as to whether the ships would be able to navigate in the heavy pack ice which surrounds the Islands. There are some who believe they could, but there has been no proof as yet. If a tanker fleet were used, it would need the support of ice-breakers.

"When the first *Manhattan* experiment took place, the United States Coastguard ice-breaker, the *North Wind*, a small ship, failed miserably, and the Canadian ice-breaker, the *John A. Macdonald*, had to come to the rescue several times. Stung by this failure, the U.S. government quickly approved the construction of an ice-breaker, the *Polar Star*, at 14,000 tons and 75,000 h.p.

"Once again the Americans took the initiative.

"Canada had the opportunity to build a polar ice-breaker at the beginning of this decade. Hearings were held by the Standing Committee on Northern Development in 1972, and Wartsila, a Finnish firm, reported that they had been retained by Humble Oil of the U.S. to do preliminary work on an icebreaker — 50,000 tons and 140,000 h.p. A similar ship could have been built by Canada at a cost of approximately $90-million, but the Ministry of Transport was not prepared to recommend the construction of such a ship unless major finds of resources were discovered in the Arctic Islands. Such discoveries in the form of natural gas had already been made, but this fact was ignored, and Canada took no steps to equip itself with an adequate ice-breaker fleet.

"Now I have some news for you, ladies and gentlemen. Just before I left my office to come to this briefing, I was informed that the *Polar Star* had been sighted this morning in the Northwest Passage off Resolute Bay."

The Chamber was filled with gasps of astonishment, followed by a burst of conversation. Even the Prime Minister had not heard the news, and immediately plunged into discussion with Robert Gendron on his right. Watts waited patiently, and as soon as the discussion petered out, proceeded.

"The ship is steaming westbound. It is very likely that her destination is Melville Island and the forcing of the McClure Strait ice which stopped the *Manhattan* in 1969. Obviously the President has directed the experimental trip to show the flag and to see how the vessel copes with the heavy ice. For your information, the United States has not asked for permission to sail through the Northwest Passage, because they maintain the position that these are high seas and not Canadian waters."

At this point the Prime Minister scribbled a note and had it delivered to Watts. He stopped, read the note, and said, " I have been informed by the Prime Minister that although my time is now officially up, I can use up the balance of the time allotted to the Minister of Defence and carry on with my presentation.

"I should also advise you that the Americans have been considering a submarine-tanker to carry crude oil or liquid natural gas from the Arctic. This is a proposal which was originally put forward by General Dynamics ten years ago. They have done a great deal of experimental work since, and are satisfied that a system could be built to pump liquefied gas into a submarine which could be docked at special under-water berths offshore. A fleet of thirty or forty of these craft could move about three billion cubic feet of gas a day from the Islands to the eastern seaboard of the United States. But once again, such a fleet does not exist, and the time factor is critically urgent for the Americans."

Watts then pushed the remote control and a new slide appeared on the screen. It was a photograph of the Resources Carrier aircraft. He went on to give details of the relationship of the Great Plains Project with Boeing, and information concerning the specifications and operational capabilities of the aircraft. He explained Canada's former control over the rights to the aircraft and its failure to participate in the research, development and construction.

"In my opinion," said Watts, "the RCA is by far the most practical way to take natural gas off the Islands. It

LARGE RESOURCE TRANSPORT AIRPLANE

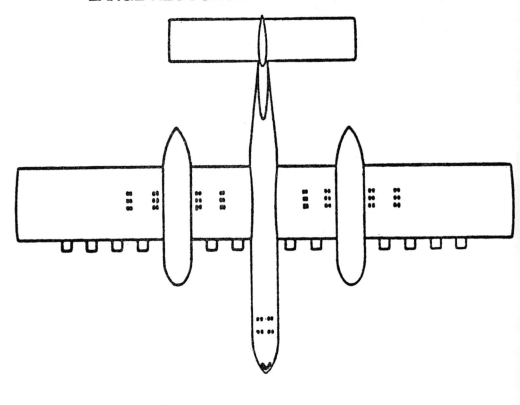

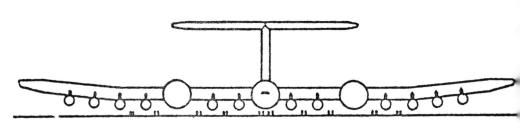

MAX GROSS WEIGHT (LB)	3,500,000
MAX PAYLOAD (LB)	2,300,000 AT 500 N.MI. RANGE
WING SPAN (FT)	478
POWER PLANT	(12) 50,000 LB SLST THRUST FANS

flies over all the difficult tundra, permafrost and mountainous terrain, and can operate in any weather. It's safe and reliable. Calculations, based on Boeing's experience with large aircraft, are that at the outside there'll be one crash per million operations, and with a single-purpose use for the craft the frequency could be even less.

"The Resources Carrier will burn natural gas, the least polluting of all fossil fuels. Landing fields will present no problem. All the Arctic Islands on which gas has been found have excellent airfield locations and approaches.

"Indications are that the aircraft can be operated for about 1½ to 2 cents per ton mile, which makes it competitive to a pipe even if a pipe could be built from the Islands. With today's prices for natural gas running at $1.25 per thousand cubic feet, there's no doubt the aircraft would be economical."

"Thirty-six Resources Aircraft would be required to transport two billion cubic feet of gas per day between the Arctic Islands and Cochrane, site of the northern end of a new LNG pipe system to New York State. If, on the other hand, Canada agrees to the United States' ultimatum and allows the Americans to come in to create their own transportation system, it is very likely that the United States will completely bypass southern Canada and move the gas directly from the Arctic Islands to key terminal points in the United States.

"It is my strong belief that the RCA system provides the United States with a practical means which is close to being operational."

Watts concluded his presentation and answered a number of questions. When he was through, he turned the lectern over to Arthur Green, Minister of the Environment.

Rat River / 8:28 a.m., MDT

The white and blue RCMP Twin Otter touched down softly in the blowing, light snow which blanketed the pipeline corridor between the scrawny jackpines. The wind was now gusting up to thirty and forty miles an hour, lifting the snow and making it difficult for the pilot to see ahead in the last few feet of his descent. But he brought it down perfectly.

They were at Rat River, the final pipeline water-crossing on Sam Allen's list.

It was near the lake where Freddie Armstrong had picked up Sam and Bessie the night before.

This would be the final defusing ordeal. By this time, having successfully completed nine attempts, Staff Sergeant Ray was relaxed and confident. As they were landing, he looked back over his long career with the RCMP.

Nothing he had ever done would compare with this. He could sure tell his boys quite a story: direct orders from the P.M., defuse the bombs, save the pipeline, save the country! They'd probably never believe him! Ray was proud. Not many men could see their whole career justified in one job.

But God! Was he tired!

Just one more of those bloody bombs and the whole thing would be finished.

He and Bessie had the defusing procedure down pat by now.

Bessie would find the package, Ray would lift it out of its hiding-place in the snow, they would lock their snowshoes together head on, then Ray would defuse the bomb.

It really was quite simple.

As the Twin Otter came to a halt, the pilot immediately put power to the engines to move it forward just slightly. He did this several times to get rid of the heat which had built up in the skis because of the friction with the snow. Otherwise, the skis would melt the snow and then freeze in, locking the aircraft solid.

Once again Ray and Bessie went through the ritual of strapping on snowshoes, getting their parkas snug to be ready to leave the aircraft.

As they made their final preparations, it was clear that Bessie, for all her strength and youth, was beginning to wilt under the strain. Ray could see it in her face and in the slow way she was moving — she was exhausted. During the entire morning she had said next to nothing, even during the tense moments of the first defusing or when it was apparent that they had successfully brought it off.

The aircraft came to a stop facing directly into the wind which was fortunately blowing straight down the Corridor from the southeast. The pilot shut the engines down.

Ray and Bessie climbed out. They were met by the high wind and blinding snow. Ray led the way, pushed along by the wind, his parka up tightly over his head. Bessie followed him closely.

They had gone only a few yards towards the watercrossing where the last bomb lay hidden in the snow when the Staff Sergeant heard Bessie moan close behind him. He turned just as she stumbled and fell into the snow. As he struggled back to her with the driven snow whipping viciously into his face, Bessie got to her knees. Then she retched and vomited.

Ray bent down, put his hands under her arms to steady her, and shouted above the wind, "Bessie, come on, I'll get you back to the aircraft."

He tried to lift her, but Bessie resisted. "No, I'll be O.K. in a minute." Her retching stopped.

Gently the Staff Sergeant helped her to stand.

He said, "Look, I can find this one by myself. You've got to get back in the aircraft where it's warm. Come on."

Bessie turned to look up at him, the snow lining her parka hood and beginning to sting her face. "Look, Jim, there's nothing wrong with me except that I'm a little bit pregnant. That's all. I'm O.K. now. Let's get this over with."

Ray gave up. He moved past Bessie and snowshoed toward the water-crossing of the Rat River where the last explosive package was to be found just at the point the enormous pipe entered the mound at the edge of the water.

Now the familiar defusing pattern began.

Bessie went up to the pipe, crouched down on her snowshoes, and gently pushed the snow from side to side until she exposed the top of a blue plastic bag. Ray lifted it out of the snow, backed off with the package until he was about ten feet from the pipe. Bessie came round in front of him, put her snowshoe in between his to form the working platform.

The two of them opened the package. Tired as he was, Ray was quite sure of himself.

Quickly he checked the timer and saw that it was O.K. They had plenty of time. He took the arming device in his left hand, then reached with the index finger of his right and firmly pushed the arming wheel away from him. At that instant he realized that he had the arming device upside down. He had twisted the arming wheel counterclockwise to detonate!

196

The bomb would blow in four seconds!

He shouted, "Run!" as he sprang to his feet, dropping the bomb beside him. Bessie turned and fled, snowshoes flailing — Ray about ten feet behind her.

Suddenly the snow-filled air was shattered by a pillar of flame and a blast that rocked and almost lifted the Twin Otter sitting a hundred yards away.

In the aircraft, with its tail toward the explosion, the young pilots could see nothing but instantly knew what had happened when the shockwave and noise of the blast hit them.

"My God! They've had it!" Sandy shouted.

Frantically, he whipped off his seatbelt, threw on his parka, opened the back door, got his snowshoes on, leaped out and raced toward the pipe — his co-pilot a few yards behind. As he reached the point of the blast, Sandy could smell, almost taste, the acrid fumes of the explosive material which still hung over the blast site despite the strong wind. Ahead of them as he raced toward the water-crossing, he could see the Staff Sergeant flat on his back with his arms outspread, and just in front of him, the figure of Bessie, face down in the snow.

He stopped and shouted to the co-pilot, "Get back to the aircraft, bring the medical kit and the stretcher. Also see if you can reach the Inuvik tower to notify headquarters. Hurry!"

The pilot went quickly over to Bessie and crouched down beside her on her right side. Very gently he lifted her head and turned it to the side, facing away from him and away from the howling wind.

Gently he brushed the snow off her face, and could see that it was unmarked. There was no evidence of blood, but under the parka and heavy trousers it could be possible she was bleeding or that her limbs were broken.

197

To check her pulse, the young constable placed his fingers on her neck. He could feel her heart beating. It was a strong beat.

As soon as the co-pilot came with the stretcher they would strap her arms to her side and lash her to two rough poles they would have to cut from the jackpines. That way, they could make sure her back was rigid when they lifted her onto the stretcher. Perhaps with any luck she might regain consciousness before they had to move her, so she could tell them if she had any pain in any particular part of her body. Already the pilot's mind was reaching back into his memory to recall the vigorous St. John Ambulance training he had been through.

Then he went over to Ray. Again there was no blood visible, but the familiar face was an ashen gray. Ray's blue eyes were wide open, vacantly staring. As the Captain put his hand under the Staff Sergeant's parka, reaching for the rib-cage immediately over the heart, he had a strong sense that he would find no trace of the pulse of life.

Clarkson, the Minister of Finance, was a little man, but he had a great deal of presence and a booming voice, so he had no trouble in holding the attention of those in the House.

He got through the usual preliminaries without delay, and then plunged immediately into facts and figures, using a chart to clarify his points. He explained that legislation enacted by the federal government to regulate the financing of the Mackenzie Valley pipeline had specified that not less than two-thirds of the ownership be in Canadian hands, while not more than 10 per cent of the funds for financing the pipe were to be obtained in Canada. "This system has worked," he said, "and the major oil purchasers of the gas in the United States, together with the U.S. government, quickly made the money available without interest until the gas started to flow through the pipe." He pointed out, however, that this deferral of interest made the investors in the United States doubly concerned when the native people began blowing up the pipeline. Undoubtedly the President was under enormous pressure from the holders of the debt to do everything in his power to force Canada to make a settlement with the native people.

Clarkson then reviewed the possible economic and trade sanctions which the United States might invoke against Canada and the counter-sanctions which Canada might employ. "Ladies and gentlemen, there is no doubt that the sanctions which can be applied against us will have disastrous short-term effects upon every individual in this country.

"I can visualize industries being shut down from coast to coast, resources extraction and processing coming to an abrupt halt and imports of foodstuffs and supplies from the United States being cut off. We would immediately have to impose rationing and price controls and establish an emergency system to feed and house thousands of people who would be without jobs.

"On the other hand, there is no doubt that the United States would suffer as well, because by counter-sanction we would cut off the 1½-million barrels of oil and the two billion cubic feet of gas per day that we supply. Furthermore, the U.S. industries which depend on our natural resources, particularly the basic minerals such as iron, nickel and copper, would be shut down until new sources of supply from offshore could be arranged, so the United States would also experience massive short-term unemployment.

"In other words, the sanctions and counter-sanctions would be harmful to the economy of both countries and would cause massive unemployment on both sides of the border. And of course, to impose drastic sanctions on Canada would be damaging to the U.S. subsidiaries in this country. I'm sure the President has considered this, but apparently he's prepared to sacrifice their interests in order to gain his objective.

"I believe that the darkest period for Canada would be the first six months after the imposition of the sanctions. By the end of that time, world opinion and world support in terms of trade and investment, and the opening of foreign markets to Canadian goods, would have taken effect and the new supply of investment capital that could be

200

obtained from Japan, the Soviet Union, Western Europe, and from OPEC would improve conditions. Nevertheless, the Canadian economy would undoubtedly have suffered a blow from which it could take us a generation to recover.

"On the other hand, if the ultimatum is accepted by Canada, no such sanctions will be imposed and no such hardships will be endured, at least so we are led to believe. Employment will be sustained, shipment of finished goods and raw materials to the United States will continue, as will the export of our precious natural gas in quantities without regard to what Canada may need for its own requirements."

Clarkson turned to his right to face the Prime Minister. "Prime Minister, strangely enough there appear to be no questions. It's now one minute to eleven. Thank you."

As Clarkson sat down, Porter rose to his feet. "Ladies and gentlemen," he said, "the special sitting of Parliament will commence at noon. His Excellency the Governor-General will open Parliament with a brief Speech from the Throne in the Senate Chamber.

"This briefing is concluded."

Ottawa / 11:10 a.m., EDT

Immediately following the briefing, the Prime Minister went directly to his office in the Main Block. He was joined by Robert Gendron, John Thomas and Tom Scott, all of whom assisted him in working out the rough draft for a brief Speech from the Throne. When they were satisfied, Porter phoned the Governor-General and discussed the speech with him. In the light of his comments, the draft was revised and the final typescript despatched by special courier to Government House. Gendron got up and prepared to leave for his own office.

"Stay and have a bite of lunch, Bob," the Prime Minister said. "Tom has ordered sandwiches and coffee for all of us."

"Thanks, but I'd better not. My name was drawn as one of those to speak in the debate this afternoon, and I've got a little over half an hour to get my thoughts on paper. I'll see you in the House."

As he left, Scott, who had gone into the outer office to pick up the lunch, came in. His face was very grave. "I have some bad news, Prime Minister. Bessie Tobac and Staff Sergeant Ray of the RCMP went out early this morning to defuse the bombs that had beet set.

"Well, sir, I don't know exactly what went wrong, but Ray must have made a slip, because the last bomb exploded on them. They seem to have known it was going to go, because they were both running, if you can run in snowshoes, but it all happened too fast. Bessie was knocked out and suffered concussion, but she seems to be O.K. She was farther away from the blast than Ray, and her heavy clothing helped protect her.

"Ray bought it immediately. He must have been crouching down to work on the bomb, because he didn't get very far. The blast broke his neck."

Porter was stunned. "Good God! Just think of the hell he must have gone through with each one of those bombs, and then to have the last one blow when he was almost home free. That's what I call a brave, brave man. I must phone his wife. I knew them when I was in Inuvik. This will be terrible for her, and they've got two teen-age boys.

"Let me know what the word is about Bessie as soon as you hear. I can tell you I'm mighty thankful she wasn't killed. She'd be a real martyr to the native people.

"Would you get a telegram off to her, Tom? Tell her how grateful we are for the risk she took and how thankful that she survived. Let me see it before you send it. Does Sam know yet?"

"No, sir. I thought it would be better if the word came from you."

"You're right. Get him on the phone for me, will you? Have the newspapers got wind of it yet?"

"Not so far as I know. The messages have come through the National Defence net by way of Inuvik Base. May I use your intercom, sir? I think I can get Sam Allen quite quickly."

The Prime Minister said, "Go ahead." Then he went back to reviewing his notes as Scott leaned across the desk and flipped the intercom switch.

"Joan, would you please get Sam Allen for me? He's at a meeting with the Deputy Minister of Indian Affairs and his Assistant."

"Yes, sir," she responded. In about two minutes the word came back. "Sam Allen on line 1, sir."

The Prime Minister picked up the phone. "Sam?"

"Yes, Bob."

The Prime Minister said, "First let me thank you for responding so quickly in coming down to start the negotiations. It's going to be tough and it's going to take time to work out, but I know I can count on you."

"I'll do my best, Bob, you know that. We've all worked hard to get to the point where our rights are recognized and an agreement can be reached. It looks to me as though we're nearly there."

"Well, stay with it. We're counting on you.

"Now, Sam, there's something else I have to tell you. I've got some bad news. Evidently Bessie and Staff Sergeant Ray got all the explosive charges defused except the last one. Something went wrong — we're not sure what exactly. Anyway it blew.

"Bessie's O.K., she's going to be fine, but Ray was killed instantly. They must have realized the explosion was coming because they'd managed to get a few feet away from the thing before it went off. Bessie got a little farther away than Ray. She was knocked out and suffered concussion, but he didn't have a chance."

Sam broke in. "Bessie's O.K.?"

"Yes, Sam, she's O.K."

"Let me tell you this, Bob. If anything had happened to her, there's no way that the native people would have settled with you or anybody else. If you think you've got problems with the Americans, I can tell you they are nothing to the problems you would have had with us if anything had happened to Bessie. Where is she?"

"She's in the hospital in Inuvik. My people will help you get through so you can talk to the doctors."

"Thanks. Bob, it seems to me if they were both trying to get away, Ray must have moved the defusing switch the wrong way. They would have had only four seconds. It's a miracle that Bessie came through. I'm sorry about Jim Ray. He was a first-rate person and a really great policeman. He did a hell of a lot for Inuvik and as much as he could for the Indians and Eskimos. I hope you can do something for his family, Bob."

"I will, Sam. I've got to get into the House shortly, so I must get back to my preparation. I just wanted to tell you myself what happened and to let you know how much I appreciate your co-operation and help."

The Prime Minister spent the rest of the hour going over the notes he had prepared earlier for his own address to the House. He jotted down the individual points on separate sheets of paper, and after he had reviewed each one passed it on to Thomas. By 11:45 he was finished. He asked his secretary to duplicate the notes on the copier and send a set to each of the other party leaders as promised.

"Send along my set of notes directly to my desk in the Commons. I've got to leave now to meet the Governor-General."

At that point Thomas said, "Bob, I've gone over all those points with you and it seems to me you've covered all the bases, but I haven't seen anything which indicates which way you're going to vote on the motion."

The Prime Minister chuckled. "I wondered when you'd ask. I've pretty well made up my mind which way I'm going to vote, John, but I decided yesterday I would give no clue in anything I wrote so that no one working with me would know and perhaps let it slip.

"Also I'm very anxious to get the results of the television and radio poll, which should be finished in just a few minutes. I'd appreciate it if you'd get hold of the President of the CBC, tell him how important it is that the information from the survey get to me in the House not later than four o'clock."

Porter held out his hand. "Thanks, John. I couldn't have got through everything without your help."

Thomas took the outstretched hand in both of his and said, "Good luck, Bob. I know the House will be behind you all the way."

The RCMP escort was waiting for the Prime Minister outside his office. They took up their position around him and once again pushed and shoved their way through the throng in the corridor. As a body they moved down to the Commons Chamber and there the escort was left behind. The Prime Minister proceeded alone, down the long centre aisle of the Chamber and then along the corridor leading to the office of the Speaker of the Senate, where he had arranged to meet the Governor-General to escort him into the Senate Chamber where the Speech from the Throne would be read.

When he arrived, the Governor-General was already in the office with the Speaker.

They shook hands, and with his usual warm smile His Excellency said, "Well, Bob, this is the moment of truth. Things have been pretty hectic. Have you been able to get as much done as you'd like?"

"Well, I think things are about as ready as I could have expected. We'll just have to hope everything goes smoothly from here on," the Prime Minister replied. Then he added, "Your Excellency, I'd be grateful if you'd stay here in the Speaker's office after you deliver the Speech from the Throne. You can watch the debate on television here. I'd like to know you're nearby while the debate is going on, so that if you have some advice to give me, all you'll have to do is send in a note. Frankly, I'd like to be able to get your opinion quickly, too."

"I'd be delighted to do that, Bob. You flatter an old man by such an expression of confidence. I'll stay here until the vote is finished and then return at once to Government House. I'll be there if you need me after that."

The two men excused themselves from the presence of the Speaker and left his Chambers. In the corridor they were met by the escort.

As they reached the Senate Chamber they were met by Senator Anderson, the Government Leader in the Senate. Everyone rose as the Governor-General entered the hall and was escorted to the Speaker's dais.

In the traditional ritual His Excellency raised his hat briefly in salute and sat down. When his audience was seated he removed the hat and handed it to the page standing behind his chair on the right.

Each time the Prime Minister had been in the Senate Chamber he had been struck by the difference between it and the House of Commons. The huge hall had a warm glow, and its handsome carpets enhanced the elaborate walnut-carved panelling of the walls. On this occasion, the room was jammed with the senators, judges of the Supreme Court of Canada and all the members of the Commons. Many of the faces of the senators were old, since the Chamber was peopled to a large extent by members of former cabinets. Other appointments were made from time to time from among outstanding Canadians, but it was an older and more august body than the Prime Minister usually faced in the Commons.

The Governor-General unrolled the scroll on which the Speech from the Throne was inscribed and began to read.

"Prime Minister, Honourable Members of the Senate, I bring you greetings from Her Most Gracious Majesty...."

In a little more than a minute, he had finished. He rose to his feet, as did everyone in the Chamber, and, accompanied by the Prime Minister who had been standing at his right, moved quickly out by the Speaker's Door.

After Porter had escorted the Governor-General back to the Speaker's Chambers and the two had exchanged a brief few words, he hurried on down the hall towards the entrance to the House of Commons. As he reached the chamber, the last of the members were making their way quickly to their seats. The premiers were in their appointed place in the Spectators' Gallery, and the balance of the Gallery was crammed with viewers.

The Prime Minister took his place. Sealed in a plastic folder on the desk were the notes that he had made earlier. As he sat down beside Gendron he asked, "Are you all set, Robert?"

"All set, Bob. Are you?"

"Oh, we Inuvikers are always ready."

The two men smiled. Except during Pierre Johnston's humorous yet convincing speech later in the afternoon, it was the last time these two men were to smile during the remainder of the day.

The room was suddenly quiet. Everyone stood as Black Rod, carrying the Mace, entered the Chamber ahead of the Speaker of the House. The Speaker mounted the dais, the Mace was placed on the table in the centre of the floor, and this most important session of the House of Commons of Canada began.

The Speaker doffed his hat to the members of the House and took his seat. Everyone sat down except the Prime Minister, who remained standing at his desk.

The Speaker recognized Robert Porter by saying, "The Right Honourable Prime Minister."

"Mr. Speaker, I have the honour to present to the House

a motion jointly put forward by the Leader of the Opposition, Mr. George Foot, the Leader of the New Democratic Party, Mr. Donald Walker, the Leader of the Social Credit Party, Mr. Pierre Johnson, and myself. It is understood, Mr. Speaker, that the motion is a formality which does not bind the movers themselves to support or reject it. It is further understood that the vote of all members shall be a free vote, so that each Honourable Member may express his opinion as his conscience dictates.

"Because of the limited time available, the leaders of the parties, other than myself, have agreed to speak on the motion for a period of twenty minutes at the opening of the debate. Each party has prepared a list — which has been placed in your hands — of those who will be entitled to speak for ten minutes each. I am quite sure, Mr. Speaker, that in the presence of this grave crisis all will adhere strictly to the time limits imposed.

"It has been agreed that, as First Minister, I shall be permitted to wind up the debate, and for that purpose will have a period of thirty minutes commencing at 4:30. The vote on the question should commence immediately after I conclude at five o'clock.

"Mr. Speaker, before I present the motion, I wish to say in your presence and in the presence of all the people of Canada who are watching or hearing these proceedings through television or radio, how profoundly grateful I am to the Honourable Leader of the Opposition and to the leaders of the New Democratic and the Social Credit parties for the non-partisan, statesmanlike attitude which each of them has demonstrated during this crisis. They have shown themselves to be true Canadians and patriots whose interest in their country and the Canadian people transcends partisan concerns in this time of emergency."

210

There was a burst of desk pounding in support of this tribute. When the din had subsided, the Prime Minister put on his glasses, picked up the sheet of paper upon which the motion was written, and said, "Mr. Speaker, with your permission I shall read the motion and then jointly move it with my honourable colleagues. It is as follows:

"Whereas the Government of the United States has issued and given to the Government of Canada an ultimatum which requires —

"(a) That the Government of Canada shall unconditionally undertake to commence negotiations toward an agreement with the native people of the Yukon and the Northwest Territories for a settlement of their aboriginal rights in terms and amounts comparable to the settlement made by the Government of the United States with the people of Alaska, and;

"(b) That the Government of Canada shall conditionally agree to grant to the Government of the United States or its designated nationals full access to the natural gas reserve discovered in the Arctic Islands, without any reservation for the future use and requirements of Canada, and;

"(c) That the Government of Canada shall unconditionally grant permission to the Government of the United States of America or its designated nationals to enter into and upon and across such Canadian territory as the Government of the United States may deem appropriate for the purpose of constructing or mounting a transportation system to carry the aforesaid natural gas from the Canadian Arctic Islands to any designated sector of the United States;

"And whereas the Government of the United States has required that an answer be given by the Parliament of

211

Canada to the aforesaid ultimatum by or before the hour of six o'clock in the evening on the date of the moving of this motion —

"Therefore this House resolves as follows:

"(1) That the aforesaid ultimatum be rejected and refused; and (2) that the Government of Canada be authorized by this Parliament to commence negotiations with the native people of the Yukon and Northwest Territories immediately to effect an equitable settlement with them in compensation for the taking of their aboriginal rights, using as a model the settlement effected between the native people of Alaska and the Government of the United States of America; and (3) that the Prime Minister of Canada be requested by Parliament to attend upon the President of the United States in Washington forthwith to open negotiations for the immediate provision to the United States of America of a sufficient quantity of natural gas from the Canadian Arctic Islands to meet both the short- and long-term requirements of the United States, subject first to the future needs of Canada, and to make arrangements for the construction and establishment of a transportation system which will make possible the movement of the aforesaid natural gas from the Canadian Arctic Islands to the United States at the earliest possible time."

The Prime Minister put down the paper from which he had been reading, slowly took off his glasses and turned to the Speaker, saying, "Mr. Speaker, that is the motion. I move its adoption."

Across the floor immediately opposite the Prime Minister, the Leader of the Opposition rose to be recognized by the Speaker. He said, "Mr. Speaker, I join in moving the motion, and to the extent that formality requires, I also second it."

He was immediately followed by the leaders of the New

212

Democratic Party and the Social Credit Party, each of whom confirmed their joint participation in the motion. When this was done, George Foot again rose and was recognized by the Speaker. He began, "Mr. Speaker, as Leader of the Opposition, and as a joint mover of the resolution, I have the privilege of leading off this debate. While the Prime Minister has made it clear that the participation of each of us in moving the motion in no way binds any one of us to support or reject it, I would like it made perfectly clear at the outset that I, as an individual Canadian, will take the position and vote in regard to the motion in the following way. . . ."

The President was in the communications cabin of Air Force One. He was facing a television set, sitting on the edge of his chair watching closely as Robert Porter read the motion in the House of Commons. When the reading was finished, he slumped back, tugged on his chin, then turned to Irving Wolf. "Irving, I've had to act the role of the tough son-of-a-bitch for the last day and a half. I'm really not very happy about it. I've a soft spot in my heart for the Canadians. They're really a mighty fine people. There's nothing sneaky about them. Whether they know it or not they're proud of their country and they've got a lot to be proud of."

He turned back to the TV set. "I really don't like putting a gun to their heads, but you and my Cabinet have advised me that this is what we should be doing and I've gone along with it."

Irving Wolf peered at the President through his black horn-rimmed glasses and said, "Mr. President, I know this is very difficult for you. Right at this moment we're at the crunch. If the Parliament of Canada accepts the motion the Prime Minister has just placed before the House then you'll have to make the next move and pronounce the sanctions which have already been agreed upon with the Cabinet and the House Leaders."

"It's those sanctions and the counter-sanctions that worry the hell out of me, Irving. We just can't afford to have the western Canadian oil and gas turned off. In the Chicago/Detroit area the energy shortage is bad enough

as it is without that. And you know if we impose investment sanctions and cut off trade to Canada, we're just
going to knock the hell out of billions of dollars' worth of
Canadian resources and manufacturing firms which are
subsidiaries of American corporations.

"It seems to me to be just too big a price to pay to get the
Canadians to come across with their natural gas. But
we've gone too far. There's no easy way back, Irving. If
they stand firm, we're all going to suffer."

Irving Wolf sat with his long nose between his two
index fingers as he thought out the President's dilemma.
Finally he said, "Mr. President, if you feel you must take
another course of action to avoid the counter-sanctions,
and at the same time save face, while ending up with an
assured supply of Arctic natural gas, I think you've no
choice but to take a hard look at the alternative plan which
you and I discussed on the weekend. I know it's perfectly
clear, but it might be helpful to you to go over the pros and
cons of it once again.

"If you decide to use it, you may wish to have it en-
dorsed by the Cabinet and government leaders when they
meet in your office at five o'clock to hear the Canadians'
decision."

Wolf dropped his hands from his face. "This is how I
think you might put the alternative plan into effect. . . ."

The President leaned back in his chair, half-closed his
eyes, and listened to Irving Wolf's line of reasoning, nod-
ding affirmatively from time to time.

As Wolf finished, the President opened his eyes and
turned to look out at the Canadian CF5's still sitting in
battle formation about a hundred yards out, watched for
a moment, then slowly turned and said, "Irving, I've no
choice but to go with the alternative."

Air Force One was high over James Bay southbound for
Washington when the decision was taken.

"I now recognize the Right Honourable the Prime Minister of Canada."

It was 4:30. The Speaker of the House had brought the long debate to a close and turned the floor over to Robert Porter. As he slowly stood up, the vast room, jammed to capacity, had a stillness as if it were empty.

"Mr. Speaker, I will be brief. I am indeed obliged to all the Honourable Members who have spoken so eloquently this afternoon. Through all their words I have detected a strong thread of sympathy and understanding for the plight of the people of the United States as they face the suffering of an energy shortage unparalleled in their history. You have witnessed this afternoon, Mr. Speaker, a most profound and understanding analysis of the bonds, the relationships, the ties which exist between our great neighbour and ourselves.

"I think it can be said, Mr. Speaker, that there has been expressed here today a fundamental recognition that Canada has a moral obligation to permit the United States reasonable access to the natural gas in the Arctic Islands and full co-operation to create a transportation system which can deliver that precious commodity to them at the earliest possible moment.

"I have said many times before, and I say again, to you this afternoon, that I share the great sympathy for the American people. And yet we must all recognize, Mr.

Speaker, the cause underlying this current crisis. The United States has permitted dangerous and unrestrained expansion of its population and its industrial complex. Per capita, the American people are by far the most prolific consumers in the world, as well as the most undisciplined. If Canada must provide the people of the United States with vast and increasing quantities of our non-renewable resources, these resources will soon be exhausted. We have every right, and indeed a profound responsibility, to demand that they take strong and far-reaching measures to conserve these resources, to place constraints upon their voracious appetite for new consumer products, and to curb the unfettered expansion of industry and market which has brought them to their current state.

"There has been a broad range of opinion expressed here today. Some members are obviously and rightly upset by the ultimatum and are clearly prepared to vote for the motion before the House. There are others who, because of the enormous sympathy they have for the people of the United States, and because they are critical of our governmental ineptitude, seem inclined to vote against the motion, but I have detected in the speches of even those members an unwillingness to give into the ultimatum without reservation.

"And so, Mr. Speaker, as I read the mood of the House, it is that the ultimatum given to Parliament by the Government of the United States should be rejected.

"Now let me turn to what the public have said about the ultimatum. As you are aware, Mr. Speaker, with the cooperation of the radio and television stations, we have been able to give the people of Canada an opportunity to express themselves for or against acceptance.

"The survey terminated at twelve o'clock noon today. At four o'clock this afternoon the President of the Cana-

217

dian Broadcasting Corporation, who was charged with the responsibility of collecting the results, delivered the final report to me. During the survey period there were 5,335,000 telephone calls. Of this number, 4,269,000 or 80 per cent, were for rejecting the ultimatum."

This announcement sparked immediate response in the audience. There was a buzz of conversation and shouts of "Hear, hear!" The Prime Minister went on.

For myself, Mr. Speaker, there is no doubt that Canada should do everything in its power at this time to assist the United States. On the other hand, I find totally unacceptable the tactics of the Government of the United States of America in forcing an ultimatum upon Canada, its largest trading partner, its closest ally, and its primary source of natural resources and raw material. Such a course is unworthy of the fundamental precepts of freedom, justice and liberty upon which that country was founded.

"Mr. Speaker, Canada must always be prepared and willing to sit down and negotiate face to face with the United States. I am ready now to go to Washington, but not under the compulsion of an ultimatum.

"Therefore, Mr. Speaker, while I fully comprehend the energy dilemma of the United States, I have no choice but to follow the lead of the members of this House and the clear indication which the people of Canada have given. I must vote in support of the motion to reject the ultimatum and to stand firm with all Canadians whatever the consequences."

For a moment after the Prime Minister sat down, the House was silent. Then there was a burst of applause. Across the aisle the leaders of the opposition parties pounded their desks in approval. In the Spectators' Galleries there was shouting and cheering.

As the Speaker called for order, the tension and expectancy of the House, which had been there unbroken throughout the afternoon, reached a new height.

"It has been agreed that there should be a recorded vote. I point out to all Honourable Members that we are somewhat ahead of schedule, as the Prime Minister has not spoken for his full allotted time. Nevertheless, I believe it is the mood of the House that we should proceed with the vote-taking immediately. Unless I receive a motion to the contrary, I shall begin.

"Mr. Clerk of the House, will you please proceed with a call of the roll."

The Clerk began, calling on each member alphabetically, without reference to party, to give his vote — yea or nay. By the time thirty members had been polled, not one vote against the motion had been recorded. At the halfway point, still no negative vote had been recorded.

As the roll call proceeded rapidly, the excited murmur became a roar. When the final vote was taken, the decision had been unanimous. The House was bedlam. The Prime Minister broke through the crush of supporters who had rushed to shake his hand or pound him on the back, and strode quickly across the floor to the Leader of the Opposition. The two embraced, and were immediately swamped by their followers.

In the Senate, a page handed a note to Senator Martinson. He signalled to the Speaker, who at once brought the debate to a close and called for a vote. When it was over, without waiting for the formality of the retirement of the Speaker, Senator Martinson rushed from the Chamber to the House of Commons to convey to the Prime Minister the unanimous support of the Senate.

Robert Porter was back in his Main Block office. With him were Gendron of External Affairs, the leaders of the opposition parties, and John Thomas. He had asked them all to join him when he informed the President formally of the decision.

While Tom Scott was placing the call, drinks were passed around. When he got through to the President's aide, he waved everyone in the room silent, and handed the telephone to the Prime Minister. "The President will be on the line in a moment, sir."

"Mr. President?"

"Yes, Mr. Prime Minister, I watched your debate on television and I know exactly what you're going to tell me. You know, we Americans think our country is mighty fine, and I must admit I admire other people who are proud of theirs. On the other hand, I think you people are a bunch of damn fools for not being prepared to do right by us at this time."

The Texas drawl became even more pronounced as the President went on. "All I can say to you, Mr. Prime Minister, is that I sure wish you'd given in, because what I must do next I don't like to have to do, but I haven't any choice now."

Porter asked quickly, "What do you propose to do, Mr. President?"

"I'm not about to tell you, son, except that I'm meeting

with my Cabinet, the leaders of the Senate and the House, and the Chief Justice and the National Security Council at 5:45. I've cleared all television and radio air time for a statement to the American people at 6:30. My suggestion, Prime Minister, is that you tune in to any television station on the Canadian network, because I'm sure they'll all pick up what I've got to say.

"There's one thing I can tell you for certain. You people aren't at a Texas tea party. You're in a Texas barroom, boy, and you'd better believe it. You'll know what I'm going to do when I speak at 6:30.

"Thank you for calling, Mr. Prime Minister. Good-bye." He hung up.

Porter had decided that the best possible place for him to be when the decision of the United States was made known at 6:30 would be Government House, so he soon made his excuses to the people in his office and went immediately to Rideau Hall. Alexander Simpson met him himself and congratulated him warmly. Then the two men went directly to the Governor-General's drawing room and settled down to watch the President's speech.

The President spoke slowly and deliberately. His face was drawn, and for the first time, he seemed tense. "My fellow Americans: Shortly after five o'clock this afternoon, little more than an hour ago, the Parliament of Canada unanimously rejected the ultimatum which I as President of the United States of America presented to the Prime Minister of Canada yesterday morning.

"Despite a full recognition by the government and the people of Canada that there is a critical energy shortage facing the United States this coming winter, and notwithstanding the fact that they know many of our hospitals, schools and factories will be shut down and many homes and apartments without electricity and heat, the Canadian government still refuses to let us have the natural gas which belongs to the American people by right of investment.

"I must point out that in rejecting the ultimatum the Canadian Parliament did make a commitment to comply with one of our demands and agreed to negotiate with the native people of the Northwest Territories and the Yukon in order to effect a settlement with them as soon as possible. I am pleased to see that the government will respond to this at least.

"Also, it is to be noted that Parliament authorized the Prime Minister to open negotiations directly with me for the purpose of ensuring that the United States obtains an adequate supply of natural gas from the Arctic Islands.

"However, in spite of the pious expression of willingness to co-operate, the rejection of our ultimatum is totally unacceptable to the United States. My administration has been dealing with the Canadians for many years now in an attempt to establish an over-all continental policy.

"These extensive negotiations have proved to be fruitless and valueless because of the inability of the government of Canada to come to a decision or to make a commitment. An undertaking to keep on negotiating, even at the highest level, is merely an undertaking to further postpone a decision.

"Time has run out. The ultimatum has been rejected, and now I have no alternative but to take a course of action which will ensure that we obtain access to the Canadian Arctic Islands gas.

"My advisers and I have been discussing the possibility of a series of economic sanctions against Canada. These can take many forms. For example, as you know, yesterday at noon I imposed an embargo on the flow of all investment funds. In addition, we can close the border to the movement of all manufactured goods and natural resource materials from Canada into the United States, with the exception of electricity, natural gas and crude oil, of course.

"It is within my power to terminate all defence-spending contracts which are now in the hands of Canadian manufacturers, and to cut off the shipment of all Canadian agricultural and food products into the American market. It is within my power to cancel the long-standing automotive free trade pact between the two countries, and there are many other sanctions which the United States could impose which would bring the Canadian economy to a halt.

"But to invoke such harsh measures would be harmful to the individual Canadian. It would be vindictive and completely out of character for the United States to take such ruthless steps. After all, we are a nation of people who cherish liberty and justice, and welcome free trade and competition. During this century we have gone to the succour and aid of people all over the world especially for the purpose of preserving the freedom of mankind against the threat of communism.

"We bear no man or nation ill, provided that nation treats our interests and our needs with honesty and fairness. But the need of the people of the United States, the need of individual American citizens for Canadian energy is imperative. It is critical, it is absolute. Canadians have a moral obligation, as our neighbours on this continent, to make this resource, which is totally surplus to Canada's own foreseeable requirements, available to us at the earliest possible moment. And yet their government will not yield.

"I cannot expect the citizens of Canada, the individual Canadian worker and his family, to suffer as a result of the selfish decision taken today by the Parliament of Canada. I cannot bring myself to impose sanctions, not only for the reason that I do not wish to see the people of Canada suffer, but also because I do not wish to see the hundreds of major Canadian subsidiaries of United States

225

corporations shut down. Nor do I wish to see the flow of natural resources, iron ore, copper, nickel, pulp and paper, from the Western Provinces cut off from the mighty American industrial complex.

"Instead, I have decided on a completely different course of action, one which will avoid the effects of a disastrous confrontation by sanction and counter-sanction. It is a course of action which should be of direct and welcome benefit to all Canadians.

"My decision has been made with the concurrence of all the members of my Cabinet and that of the leaders of both parties in the Senate and the House of Representatives. It will provide all the Canadian people with a better opportunity to share their massive resources with us, and in exchange to participate directly in the high standard of living and superior citizenship enjoyed by the people of the United States.

"As of this moment, Canada will become part of the United States of America. The Government of Canada is hereby dissolved. The provinces will become full member states of the Union. All necessary legislation will be presented to Congress to implement this decision.

"To ensure that this transfer of power takes place smoothly and without incident, transport aircraft and helicopters of the United States Air Force carrying troops and equipment are now landing at airports in all major Canadian cities and at all Canadian Armed Forces bases.

"I hereby instruct the Governor-General of Canada, as Commander-in-Chief of the Canadian Armed Forces, to instruct the Chief of the Defence Staff to order his forces to lay down their arms and to co-operate fully with our troops.

"The citizens of Canada are now citizens of the proudest, finest, greatest nation in the world. To all of you we give

226

the gift of citizenship in the United States of America.
I want every one of you to be proud of this new gift, and
I bid each of you welcome, my fellow Americans."

*The Governor-General reached over and lightly touched
Robert Porter on the arm.*

*"Well, Bob, it appears we have no choice. We fought for
our independence as long as possible, but it couldn't last.
My last act as Governor-General must be to follow the
instructions of the President."*